WHEN FRIENDSHIP followed ME HOME

a novel by
PAUL GRIFFIN

DIAL BOOKS FOR
YOUNG READERS

Dial Books for Young Readers
Penguin Young Readers group
An imprint of Penguin Random House LLC
375 Hudson Street
New York, NY 10014

Printed in the United States of America
ISBN 9780803738164

1 3 5 7 9 10 8 6 4 2

Design by Jasmin Rubero
Text set in Aldus LT Std

Pages 8 and 149: Quotes from *Feathers* by Jacqueline Woodson,
copyright 2007 by Jacqueline Woodson.
Used by permission of G. P. Putnam's Sons Books for Young Readers,
an imprint of Penguin Young Readers Group,
a division of Penguin Random House LLC.
Photo on page V courtesy of Library of Congress, Prints & Photographs Division,
Detroit Publishing Company Collection [LC-DIG-det-4a12420]
Photos on pages 36 and 47 by Risa Morimoto

This is a work of fiction. Names, characters, places, and incidents either are the product
of the author's imagination or are used fictitiously, and any resemblance to actual persons,
living or dead, businesses, companies, events, or locales is entirely coincidental.

For Risa, with all my love and thanks for letting me travel time with you.

AND

For John, kid brother, superhero.

LUKE SKYWALKER: What's in there?

YODA: Only what you take with you.

STAR WARS, EPISODE V: THE EMPIRE STRIKES BACK

1

CHUNKY MOLD

You'd have to be nuts to trust a magician. I learned that lesson the hard way. And then, if you can believe it, I actually became a magician's assistant. That part was the Rainbow Girl's fault, but the rest of it I blame on a little dog named Flip.

The trouble started the second Friday of seventh grade. Damon Rayburn shoved me out of the lunch line. "Thanks, Coffin," he said.

"For what?" I said.

"Offering to buy me a slice."

If you think a little threat like that could get me to surrender my pizza money to an idiot like Damon Rayburn, you know me pretty well. He slapped the back of my head and cut to the front of the line.

"You're half a foot taller than him, Coffin," this kid half a foot shorter than Rayburn said. His name was Chucky Mull, but everybody called him Chunky Mold. "You should have belted him. Now he knows he can push you around."

"Allow me to quote Yoda, from *The Empire Strikes Back*,"
I said. "'A Jedi uses the Force for knowledge and defense,
never for attack.'"

"You were being called upon to defend your inalienable
right to eat meatball pizza," Mold said. "Yoda also says don't
be a wimp."

"Yoda never uses the word *wimp*."

"He says, 'Fear is the path to the dark side.' Dude, hello,
The Phantom Menace?"

There was no debating Mold on this stuff. He had the
T-shirts—the sheets too. I shoved him toward our spot far,
far away in the dark corner where they kept the garbage
dumpster nobody ever dumped. Mold's mom had stuck a
note on the waxed paper that barely covered his foot-long
hero. It said, LOVE YOU. ☺ He tossed the note and crammed
a hunk of sandwich into his mouth. "Any chance you would
consider splitting that with me?" I said. "Come on, Mold,
you'll never be able to finish the whole thing."

"Watch me," Chucky said. "Holy crud, here she comes."

Mrs. Pinto worked her way toward us. She was really pretty
for a principal or even a normal human being. "Hi guys," she said.

"Good, how are you?" Mold said.

"If you ever need anything, stop by my office, okay?"

"You too," Mold said.

Mrs. Pinto patted my shoulder as she left.

"She totally just touched you," Chucky said. "You, a loser,

caressed on your loser shoulder by Mrs. P. I sent her the wink almost like four hours ago now. Nothing. Why are you staring at me like that? Dude, the emoticon? Are you visiting from The Stone Age?"

"I know what the wink is. I just can't believe you sent her one."

"So?"

"She's old. Mold, she's like *thirty*."

"It's not what you think. On Facebook the wink is a sign of supreme respect. It's like when somebody inspires you, you wink at them. It's true. It's an ancient custom that goes all the way back to classical times, the Greeks and Romanians. It's like you're bowing to her to acknowledge her awesomeness."

"Then why not just send her a bow?"

"Because there's no emoticon for that, you moron. Just because she has a totally amazing butt doesn't mean she can't be my hero too, for her, you know, incredible wisdom and everything."

"*That's* why you winked at her—her *wis*dom."

"What do you know anyway? You're not even on Facebook. It's a real thing, I swear. In many cultures it's considered rude *not* to send the wink." He batted away a fly from where the peanut butter slimed his lip like a gluey booger.

I had to believe him, firstly because you can tell when somebody's lying, and he truly didn't think he was, and most of all because he was right about me not being on Facebook. The whole *friends* thing: It wasn't really happening. Even Mold was more aggravation than ally. I moved to the neighborhood less than two years before. In a year me and my mom were heading to Florida, right after she retired. We could live great down there for cheap, she said. I figured why bother making friends when I was out of here pretty soon?

"Chucky, not even a bite? Really?" I said.

"Dream on," he said, or something like that. I couldn't tell with the sandwich all gunked up in his braces.

2

HEIR TO THE EMPIRE

My stomach was growling by the time the last bell rang and they set us free for the weekend. I headed down the boardwalk toward the library. Mrs. Lorentz always kept a plate of Chips Ahoy! at the front desk.

I was feeling pretty terrific for somebody who got robbed of his pizza money. You can't be sad in Coney Island on a clear September day. The ocean was glittery. The air smelled salty and sweet. My audiobook was nearing the climax. I couldn't get caught walking around with a *book* book, of course. That's like begging for a wedgie. I cranked up my headphones and *Heir to the Empire,* by Timothy Zahn. Things were looking crummy for Han Solo. Thrawn's fighters swarmed the *Millennium Falcon.* The sound cut out when somebody came up behind me and ripped the headphones off my head.

"Who buys yellow headphones?" this girl Angelina Caramello said. She was really pretty even though she was friends with Damon Rayburn. "It's like lemons growing out of your ears."

"Plus you missed a belt loop," Angelina's best friend Ronda Glomski said. She yanked on the loop I missed. "I truly don't understand how you got skipped a grade. How can you be so lame yet so totally adorbs?"

"Ew," Angelina said. She chucked my headphones at me. Then Ronda shoved me so hard she knocked the gum out of my mouth.

I had to think about this. Ronda Glomski, ranked eleventh prettiest in our grade, said that I, Ben Coffin, was not totally revolting. Even though she practically decked me right after she said it and her name was a little gross sounding. I know, like I should talk when my name reminds you of where a zombie escaped from. We were kind of perfect for each other if you took out the part about Ronda being really mean.

In my side vision I saw Damon Rayburn coming, which meant I had to be going, and fast.

I was wheezing a little by the time I got to the library. It wasn't that far a sprint, but my asthma was kicking in, and I had forgotten my inhaler. Fortunately Mrs. Lorentz had it. "You left it on the windowsill again," she said. She pushed a book at me. "I need you to read this. My daughter can't stop talking about it. I'm looking for a second opinion before I put it on top of my stack."

It was *Feathers*, by Jacqueline Woodson. "This doesn't look like sci-fi," I said.

"You won't spontaneously combust," Mrs. Lorentz said. "Ben, you'll love it, trust me."

"After you just said you haven't read it?"

"Why are you standing here talking to me when you should be reading?"

"It's written by a girl," I said.

"So?"

"Like, I'm a dude."

"Take some cookies with you, *dude*. And yes, you can keep the fire escape door open a crack."

She let me do that on asthma days. The breeze felt nice. I didn't know it just then, but getting stopped by Angelina and Ronda, which led to me getting chased by Rayburn, which got my asthma going, which made me crack the alley door, was about to flip my life upside down.

I propped open the door with one of the grimy old encyclopedias Mrs. Lorentz was always trying to dump on everybody—Volume 10, Gargantuan to Halitosis—and settled in at my table hidden away in the back. There were all these giant pictures silkscreened onto the walls, photographs from the old days when Coney Island was the most famous beach in America. My favorite was called *Dreamland at Night*. It was the way Luna Park, this amusement park right on the ocean, looked in 1905. The tower shined like a softer sun. Think of honey lit up with the kind of electricity inside an angel's mind when she's wishing only the most beautiful things for you.

I took a breath from my inhaler and eyed *Feathers*. The cover was a picture of, guess what, a feather. No spaceships, no exploding Death Star, not even a freaking laser sword. The story went like this: There's this new kid in school. Some call him the Jesus Boy, others think he's a freak and they bully him bad. I related to him. I'm not talking about the bullying but about how I always felt like a stranger, even to myself sometimes. I just didn't know where I fit in or what I was supposed to do or be in life, like maybe I was a mistake.

Pretty soon I was on the last page of the book. The story was the kind that ends too quick and leaves you worrying about what's going to happen to the characters, almost like they're your friends, except not annoying. Frannie, the narrator, wants to be a writer. Her teacher is telling her that each day comes with its own special moments and that Frannie had better keep an eye out for them and write them down for later. I was okay with that part. I'm sure Timothy Zahn did that kind of stuff when he was writing *Heir to the Empire*. But I had to stop when I read the next thing Frannie's teacher said about these so-called special moments. "Some of them might be perfect, filled with light and hope and laughter. Moments that stay with us forever and ever."

This was a lie. Nothing lasts forever. It's a scientific fact. Things happen and they're over and you can't get them back.

Einstein said we can travel to the future, and the astronauts proved it. They synchronized twenty clocks and took ten into space. They spent six months up there, whipping around at 17,000 miles an hour, almost five miles per *second*. When they landed, *all* the clocks in Mission Control were .007 seconds ahead of *all* the ones that went into space. You see what happened? They traveled a fraction of a second into the future. Look it up if you don't believe me. This means if you travel *really* fast, like at light speed, when you land back on Earth the clocks will be *years and years* ahead, and you've escaped far into the future. Here's the problem: Einstein used the same math to prove we can never go back to the past.

I stared into the picture of Luna Park in 1905. I would never get to be there. I'd never feel safe with all those gold and silver lights on my face. I'd never see the world from the top of the tower. I'd never believe magic was real.

A cat hissed outside the fire escape door. It charged something down the alley. Then came that creepy sound a cat makes when it's mad, like a demon possessed it.

3

THE DEMON, THE DOG
AND THE DIVA

I stepped into the alley. The cat was beating the heck out of this other, much smaller one, except the little guy was a dog.

I shooed away the cat. The dog was a shivering mess. His fur was all tarred up. His tongue stuck out the side of his mouth. His eyes were gunky and pointed out toward the sides. His tail was chomped up and bent, what I could see of it. He had it between his legs. What a shrimp he was. He weighed maybe eight pounds. He wasn't young either, with the gray in his muzzle. I went to pet him. He ducked and scampered out of the alley. I tried to find him, but he was gone.

I brought *Feathers* back to Mrs. Lorentz. "So?" she said.

"It makes me upset."

"That's great," she said.

"*Great?*"

"Why does it upset you, Ben?"

"I'm not sure. Can you hold it for me?"

"You don't want to take it home?" she said.

"I forgot my backpack today."

"It weighs four point five ounces, not to mention its title is *Feathers*. You can't *carry* it?"

I looked out the window. A bunch of guys were hanging out by the free newspaper boxes everybody throws garbage in. They'd take *Feathers* and rip it up, and then Frannie and the Jesus Boy would be in pieces, getting kicked around in the wind. "How do you know it weighs four point five ounces?" I said.

"I'm guessing." She dropped the book onto a postage scale: 4.5 exactly.

"You're not human," I said.

She nodded and leaned in and whispered, "I'm a librarian." She wrote on a sticky paper and stuck it to the book. Then the weirdest thing happened. Her lips trembled and I swear she was about to cry. "Don't forget your inhaler," she said as she put the book aside to help this other kid check out a stack of video games. I leaned over the counter to see what she wrote. The note said: HOLD FOR MY BEN.

I was going to miss her next year, when Mom and I moved to Miami. It almost made me want to join Facebook, the idea that if I didn't, I'd never see her again. I would send her the biggest wink, Mrs. Lorentz, to acknowledge all the kindness she showed me the past two years, not to mention her totally amazing wisdom. I'd send her the wink every freaking day.

I was heading out when this girl was coming in. I held the door for her. She wore a lime-green beret, oversized sunglasses, a glittery scarf, and a red suit jacket with gold buttons buttoned up to her neck, even though it was like seventy-five degrees out. She wore purple gloves with the fingers cut off. Her high-tops were pink sparkles. She pretty much had every color of the rainbow covered. Her backpack was one of those mesh ones so she could show you how totally brilliant she was with all the books she had in there.

The big bad tough guys outside didn't mess with her—no sir. She was the kind of girl who, if you cracked some lame comment about her books or *gloves* or whatever, she'd come back with something that made you feel even stupider than you are, and in front of all your buddies too. Even the dumbest guy knows not to mess with a diva.

And boy, was she one. She stopped to check a text. Here I am, holding the freaking door for her, and the whole time she's texting back. And then she brushed right past me without even tossing me a thanks.

"You're *wel*come," I said. No I didn't. I just left.

It was five thirty. Mom liked me home by six to help with dinner. The tide was coming in. The salt smell was strong enough to make you cough. Papers blew around the street. I had a feeling I was being followed.

I turned around. Mermaid Avenue was packed with everybody coming home from work, but nobody seemed interested in me. I headed up to Neptune, which was a little less crowded, and now I was sure somebody was stalking me. I spun around, and there he was.

4

THE STALKER

That little dog from the alley stopped maybe fifty feet away and sat and watched me.

"C'mere then," I said, but he wouldn't. I walked toward him and he ran off. I shrugged and went on. I looked over my shoulder, and he was following me again.

I went into the supermarket to where the lady in the hairnet was always trying to push the free cheese samples on you. "Can I have some?" I said.

"What else am I here for?" she said.

I scooped four fistfuls into my pockets.

"At least tell your mom the cheese was good," the lady said. "You know, so maybe she *buys* some next time?"

"Oh, I will."

"*Right*," she said. I felt bad for her. Selling fancy cheese in a mediocre supermarket is a hard job.

When I came back out, the dog was waiting for me. He was

closer now, and boy was he shaking. I put a piece of cheese on the sidewalk and stepped back twenty feet. He approached real slow, and then he gobbled it. I put another one down and stepped back ten feet this time, and it was the same thing. Then five feet, then he was eating out of my hand. I swear he wolfed down a quarter pound of cheddar. He let out a burp louder than any I ever made. His breath was not particularly fantastic. Then he leaned into my leg and shook so hard he shook me.

I scooped him up and took a quiet side street home. No way was I getting caught carrying around a girly little dog like that. It would have been worse than being caught with a book.

5
MOM

"The answer is yes," my mother said. I didn't even get a chance to ask her. She just saw the little varmint in my arms and said okay. "Now let's get this dog into the tub."

"Thanks, Mom." I'd wanted a dog for as long as I could remember, but we were going to wait until we got to Florida. Luckily, Mom liked to go with the flow.

"He picked you for a reason," she said.

"Right, I'm the first sucker who fed him."

She messed up my hair. "Life's a journey, Traveler."

"And we're all in for one heck of a ride."

"Hiking uphill is the best part of the trip, never forget," she said.

"How could I when you remind me twice a day?"

She was sixty-seven years old. She didn't dye her hair, which she kept short, no fuss, no muss. You might be doing the math, her age minus mine, a seventh grader's. She'd have to be in her mid-fifties when she had me, right? Except she didn't. I was ten when she took me in.

"Get the towel," Mom said.

We dried him off, and wouldn't you know that little mutt was sort of cute. His coat was spiky. With the gunk gone his eyes were gold brown. I tucked his tongue into his mouth, but it fell out.

"Let's fatten him up," Mom said.

Her saying yes to the dog so quick got me thinking. "Mom, all those kids in the group home. You could have adopted any of them. I've always been afraid to ask, but why me?"

"Why were you afraid to ask?" She started frying up some hamburger.

"Sometimes I think if I talk about it, it'll disappear. Living here, in the apartment. My own room. Dinner while we watch TV. You and me."

"Traveler?" she said. "You and I will never disappear. We're forever. You know that, don't you?"

"Of course."

"You're a terrible liar, son."

"How do you know I'm lying?"

"Because you do this adorable little thing with your eyes. They open a bit too wide, and you look off to the right. Ben? It's like this: When Laura died so suddenly I was at a crossroads. We'd always talked about becoming foster caregivers, and I thought, well, if I find the right kid, the one who really needs *me*, I'm going to do it." She stopped cooking to look at me full on. "I just knew you were meant to be my son."

"How'd you know, though?"

"Magic." She wasn't talking to me now. She looked past me, at the picture on the wall above the kitchen table. Mom's partner Laura watched over us every night as we ate. She had a true smile, like she wasn't forcing it for the picture. She got cancer, the kind that hijacks your blood. "She would have loved you," Mom said. Then she snapped out of it and got back to cooking. "There's not much here. You'll be hungry. You'd better go pick up some Chinese food." Now *she* was lying. There was plenty of hamburger, even with the dog there, but I saw she wanted to be alone for a bit. She didn't like to be sad in front of me.

"Mom? They have this new cheddar at the supermarket. It's really terrific."

"Good to know. Hey, our new friend here, what are you going to call him?"

"Not sure yet."

"You'll know when you hear it."

I made a leash from my bathrobe belt, but I didn't need it. That little dog trotted right alongside me, all the way to the Palace of Enchantment and back, and he never once took his eyes off me. Even when he was eating he wouldn't stop staring at me. After dinner when we watched *Star Trek II: Wrath of Khan,* it was the same way, eyes on me the whole time. He had a thing about him that was hard to describe. Like this very golden stillness. His name had to show that.

"Why are you smiling?" Mom said.

"I don't know," I said, but I knew. It was so perfect, just plain old hanging out, Mom, me and the dog. It was so safe. "Maybe we could call him Woody."

"As in Woody Coffin?"

"Right, scratch that."

"Coffin's a tricky name," she said.

"It's awesome. Remember how you said I could stay a Smith if I thought Coffin was too creepy?" There were lots of Smiths in the foster homes, and Joneses and Washingtons. "That was the best, the day you let me share your name."

"That was a beautiful day. Yes, it was."

"I just felt different, like finally I was getting a little closer to becoming the person I was supposed to be, even if I didn't know exactly who that person was yet."

"I like that you tell me these things. Oh, don't be embarrassed now. Ben, your friend is trying to get your attention."

The little guy had slid out of my lap and trotted to the door. He put up his paw and yipped, just once. I took him out and he peed right at the curb. When bedtime came he wriggled under my shirt, into my armpit. I woke up to check on him, and his head was resting on my chest. He was looking at me with those gold-brown eyes. It occurred to me that I hadn't taken a breath from my inhaler since the library, and I was breathing fine. I ran my fingers through his coat, back and forth, and like no hair came off him. My lungs were cool around dogs who didn't shed a lot. "You're awesome," I said. He dove at my mouth and licked my lips. "Except for that breath. Whoa."

When I woke up the next morning he was checking out the Chewbacca poster I'd tacked up by my bookcase. It was life-size—seven feet of Wookie staring right at you. The little mutt cocked his head, like, Dude, you are the weirdest dog I've ever seen.

6

THE MICROCHIP

"His teeth are in decent shape, which means he was well cared for," the veterinarian said.

"Then how'd he end up on the street?" I said.

The vet shrugged. "Maybe he was a companion animal for an elderly person. She dies, the family drops him at a shelter. From there, let's say he's adopted by people who had good intentions but no time to care for him. The dog gets dumped again. Or . . ."

"Or?"

"Maybe he's just lost. He has a microchip embedded in his skin. Look." The doctor passed a scanner over the dog's shoulder. A phone number came up on the iPad screen. "That's his owner. There's an email address too."

"Maybe he ran away," I said. "She was probably treating him really rotten."

"Traveler?" Mom said. "Think how you would feel if you lost your dog. Think about the dog most of all. It's in your power to reunite him with the person who cared for him all these years."

My power, huh? I wasn't feeling very powerful. I was feeling like I wanted to barf all over the vet's office.

We plunked down on the bench outside the veterinarian's and waited for Mom's sister, Jeanie. We were hitching a ride with her to the Bay Ridge mall. The website said you could bring your dog inside the pet supply store, except he wasn't really my dog now. I took out my phone, hit speaker and dialed.

Mom chucked her arm over my shoulder. "I'm proud of you," she said.

The dog was snoring in my lap. Then came the voice. *The number you are trying to reach has been disconnected.*

Mom nudged me. "We're halfway home. There's still that email address, Traveler."

"Mom—"

"Send it off, and we have a clear conscience we did everything we could."

I tapped the email into my phone with a message to call our home number. I forced myself to hit send right as Aunt Jeanie pulled up. Her boyfriend Leo leaned out the window. "First a kid and now a dog, huh Tess? Better you than me." He laughed like it was the best joke ever. He got out with Aunt Jeanie to help Mom into the car. She had a touch of the arthritis. "I'm *fine*," she said. "You're such a gent, Leo, but I'm not an invalid—yet."

"You'll outlast all of us, sweetheart," Leo said.

"I certainly hope not. Ben, give your aunt a hug."

Jeanie was nice and all, but when she hugged you, she pushed you away the slightest bit, like you'd better not mess up her makeup. She worked as a manager at Macy's, and she got a huge discount at the cosmetics counter. She was younger than Mom but looked older. The skin around her eyes wrinkled out like spiderwebs, probably because she was always squinting and scrunching up her forehead the way you do when you get worried. She came over to the apartment now and then. "Tell me about school, are you doing any sports, are boys really wearing their hair that long now?" She wasn't nasty or anything. More like she was just, I don't know, a little *nervous* being around me. Leo I didn't know so well. I'd see him holidays, for dinner or whatever. He was a little over-friendly, like he'd shake your hand all exaggerated and slap your shoulder and practically yell, "Hey, how the heck are ya?" Except he didn't wait for you to answer, and then he was running back to the TV to watch the game. I'd watch with him and I swear he'd say it fifty times, "Have some chips, champ. Put a little meat on those bones." I always wanted to tell him that chips weren't made of meat. They were made of freaking *kale,* if Aunt Jeanie had her way. She was kind of a health food freak. I don't know. Leo was okay, I guess.

We got into the backseat of Aunt Jeanie's Mercedes. There was a sheet over it. "Will he stay back there, the dog?" Jeanie said. "I can't have all that fur everywhere, Tess."

"And good morning to you on this gorgeous Saturday, sister darling," Mom said. She kissed Jeanie's cheek, then Leo's.

"Sorry," Jeanie said. "It's just that I had the car vacuumed yesterday."

"Babe, relax," Leo said. He winked at me. "Right champ?"

The dog nudged my hand and put up his paw.

"He wants you to give him a high five," Mom said.

I gave him a knuckle bump and he dove at my face and licked my lips.

"Whoever had him before trained him well," Mom said.

"Totally. I really hope she's dead," I said.

"Well, Traveler, I'm not particularly thrilled by that sentiment."

At the mall we picked out a leash and collar and this pet carrier backpack so you could take him with you on the train. It was like that diva girl's mesh backpack except sturdy. The little guy didn't mind the pack at all. The cashier dropped a chew stick in there and the dog hopped right in after it. The pack was half off, but it was still expensive. "Should we wait until we're sure he's ours?" I said.

"We'll give it to his owner, if it comes to that," Mom said. "And if she doesn't want it, we'll have it for when we get another dog."

"Another dog," I said. "Sure."

7

THE MOLD HORDE

"He's totally part Ewok," Mold said.

"Teebo, right?" I said.

"More like Wicket. That's what you should call him."

"How about Spidey?" I said. "Flash?"

"Wicket's cooler. Or Gandalf."

"No way."

"Potter?"

"No magicians," I said.

"Dude, chill, no need to be racist about it. C'mere, little guy. Coffin, he is *awe*some. My sisters are going to flip."

We climbed the stairs to his porch. I'd never been to his house but knew it from half a block away by the bent light saber in the driveway and the kiddie pool filled with green-brown water. The peekaboo window alongside the front door was patched with cardboard from a Dr Pepper box. Inside, barefoot kids ran all over the place.

"Mom, this is Coffin," Chucky said. "He's my friend, sort of."

"Hello Coffin." She hugged me. She smelled like cookies, and she was a good hugger all right. I couldn't breathe.

"I *love* him," this like four-year-old girl said. She had a peanut butter beard and jelly splotches on her nightgown. The dog went straight to licking the peanut butter off her lips. A horde of other girls in nightgowns joined in. Not in licking off the peanut butter. In cuddling the dog, I mean. One of them was crawling around with a loaded diaper. The dog found that terrifically interesting.

An old golden retriever limped into the swarm. The dogs sniffed each other's butts. The retriever lay down, and my dog—maybe—settled in next to her. Their tails beat the dust from the carpet. All of a sudden my dog jumped and begged me to pick him up.

A scrawny old cat came into the room, sat and licked its butt hole in front of everybody. Now I knew why I was having trouble breathing. The cat hair was all over Mrs. Mold's nightgown and everyone else's. Only certain kinds of dogs made my throat itch, but cats got me wheezing every time. And why was everybody in nightgowns at three in the afternoon?

"Ginger *loves* dogs," Mrs. Mold said. "Ears, GinGin. Ears."

The cat licked the wax out of the retriever's ears and the dog sighed happily.

"Ginger can clean Fuzzball's ears too, if you want," Mrs. Mold said.

"I think his ears are totally okay," I said. I left out the part about wasn't the cat's tongue just up its butt? Mrs. Mold took the dog out of my arms. The cat went straight at my dog's ear with her slimy tongue, and my dog stopped shivering and started thumping.

"That means he *loves* it," one of the littler kids said. "The other way you know they're happy is they hump you."

"It's true," Chucky said.

"Stay for pizza, Coffin," Mrs. Mold said.

"Do we have enough?" Chucky said.

"*Yes*, Charles, we only have about a billion boxes in the cellar freezer."

"Sorry, bud," Chucky said, "it's just that living around here, I have resource allocation concerns. I acknowledge that I have a problem, and I'm dealing with it."

I couldn't breathe but I was famished. Air or food?

We had burnt frozen pizza, and it was awesome.

8

THE UNDERWEAR THIEF

Monday morning I took the dog with me on my coupon delivery route. A lady in a housedress came out of nowhere and hit me with a broom when I left a pennysaver at her door in front of a sign that said DO NOT LEAVE SALES MATERIALS OF ANY KIND. My boss told me to ignore those signs especially. "Sorry ma'am, just following orders," I said.

"See if you can follow them after I beat your brains in." She swung the broom at my rear end.

That little dog rolled over at the lady's feet and wagged his crooked tail. The lady forgot about me and scratched the dog's belly. She was a whole different person now, like actually *nice*. She invited us in for a bagel, but I had to get to Health and Safety class, where Rayburn nailed me with spitballs. Avoiding him the rest of the day was no problem because, well, let's just put it this way: He wasn't in Honors. I ate lunch under the stairs.

After school I ran home. I'd set up my phone with the

camera on time lapse to see what the dog got up to. Here's what he did all day after Mom went to work: Nothing, except he got into my laundry basket and grabbed hold of my underpants. He made a pillow of them in the hallway and sighed, eyes on the door the whole time, until—and this was crazy—he went insane scratching at the door five minutes before I even put the key in, like he had ESP that I was on my way home.

I checked my email. Still no word from the dog's previous owner. She was dead for sure. I was feeling really, really terrific about everything.

"You got a dog, right?" Mrs. Lorentz said.

"How do you know these things?" I said. I turned around so she could see the dog through the mesh panel of the backpack.

"You don't swamp the online reservation system with requests for dog training books when you adopt a ferret. Come around back here and let me see."

I went behind the main desk, put the backpack on the floor, and unzipped it.

"I want to eat him," Mrs. Lorentz said.

"*Why?*"

She scooped him up. "Hel*lo*, you little wombat." The dog attacked her with a kiss. I mean he like totally Frenched her. "His eyes," she said. "They remind me of our little guy

Harry. We lost him in June. He was old. Died in his sleep in my daughter's arms. You can't wish for a better good-bye-for-a-while than that, right?"

"Good-bye-for-a-while," I said. "Sure."

An old man came to the counter to return a laptop. His book bag said: READING MAKES YOU LIVE LONGER. JUST LOOK AT ME.

Mrs. Lorentz put the dog into my backpack. She nodded to a stack on the counter. "Those are yours, Ben." On top of the dog training books was *Feathers*. When I turned to put the books into the backpack, the dog was gone.

9
RETURN OF THE RAINBOW GIRL

The little mutt trotted to the back of the library where the diva was camped out. She wore a yellow beret, fluorescent pink nail polish and a tangerine scarf. The only thing not popping bright about her was her skin, which was really pale. She had bags under her eyes too, like she stayed up the whole night reading all those books I saw in her backpack last time. The dog climbed into her lap. "It's criminal, his adorableness," she said. "What's his name?"

"Not sure yet," I said. "I've only had him three days."

She'd spread her books out all over the table that was previously mine until she took over the entire freaking thing. One was a copy of *Feathers*. Crazy-colored sticky notes marked off the pages.

"You're her," I said. "Mrs. Lorentz's daughter." The book was in my hand, *Feathers*, the library copy. "I'm almost done reading it."

"Some books change the way you see the world, and then there's the one that changes the way you breathe. How are you loving it?"

"You know, totally."

"Then you may sit," she said. She gave the dog a belly scratch. "I love how his tongue sticks out the side of his mouth."

"How come I've never seen you around here before?" I said.

"I just started homeschooling. I work in my apartment until lunch, but after that I get totally stir-crazy. Besides, you have seen me before."

"You mean on Friday when you made me hold the door for you the whole time you texted your friend back?"

"Before that, and sorry for being preoccupied. I was in the middle of a pretty important exchange. You really don't remember me?"

It took me a little while to remember that I actually had met her. The oversized beret covering her head threw me off, but she was the girl with the loopy light brown hair from last winter break. "You helped me check out my books while Mrs. Lorentz was on the phone," I said.

"Who admits to having read *I, Robot* and then *renews* it?"

"You look—"

"Different," she said. "Look closer. See?" She had practically no eyebrows. "The chemotherapy is actually working.

My latest bloods and scans are looking pretty decent. Bad numbers down, good ones up. I'm totally going to kick this thing's butt, you know?"

"I know," I said, like an idiot, like I knew anything about her except she made me feel the way I did when I saw the dog following me but afraid to follow me. It was like when Darth Vader chops off Luke Skywalker's hand. Vader will let Luke live if he joins the dark side, but Luke doesn't. He doesn't submit to Vader's light saber either. He freaking jumps into a reactor. The Force is with him, though, and he falls into a garbage chute, and after that Leia rescues him, and he gets a totally cool bionic hand. Yeah, this girl was tough like that.

"That was the email I got when you were starring in the role of aggrieved doorman," she said. "The old thumbs-up from the doc. Yeah. I'm one of the lucky ones. The side effects from the chemo aren't totally awful, other than I get tired for a few days after. And of course the, like, hair thing." She nodded, and that got me nodding, despite the fact I was totally confused. It just made zero sense. You don't take medicine that makes your hair fall out unless you're *really* sick, and she was my age.

"Anyway, it's just hair," she said. "And it grows back, just so you know."

"You still look totally beautiful, though," I said. Sometimes I want to punch myself in the mouth, except it would hurt and just make me look even stupider. "Sorry, I have this problem sometimes where I forget not to say what I'm thinking."

"How is that a problem, and why would you ever apologize for saying I'm totally hot?"

"Excuse me, *beautiful* I said."

"That's twice now." She reached across the table and squeezed my hand, just for a second. "Thanks," she said. Her fingers were cold and covered in sparkly gel ink. So was the top page of her spiral notebook, with the prettiest script, starbursts instead of dots over her *j*'s and *i*'s. "I'm writing a novella," she said.

"Seriously?"

She made her face overly serious. "I'm afraid so. You're not a writer?"

"I'm twelve."

"Then what are you waiting for? My mom thinks you're really cool, by the way."

"She's totally wink-worthy," I said.

"Ex*cuse* me?"

"No, like on Facebook, you know? The wink? I'd totally send her the hugest one."

"Ew." She packed up her books.

"I'm getting the feeling the wink doesn't mean what I think it means," I said.

She tapped up this blog about Facebook etiquette and appropriate use of emoticons. Here's what it said:

;o) also known as "the wink," is totally okay from your
boyfriend, totally *not* in most other cases, and totally *ick*
from the creep who thinks you're hot when he's so not.

"Wow," I said.

"Yah." She wasn't too tired that day, the way she was
marching for the exit.

I leashed the dog and scooped up the books Mrs. Lorentz
left at the main desk for me and shoved them into the backpack.

"Why'd she storm out like that?" Mrs. Lorentz said.

"*No* idea." I couldn't even look at her.

The dog and I caught up with the Rainbow Girl on the
side street. She was heading for the boardwalk. "You'll never
guess what I thought the wink meant," I said.

"I don't want to know," she said.

"Anyway, I didn't think it meant what it *means.*"

"I know," she said. "I overreacted. I do that. It's just one
of the many facets that make up the intricate gem that is my
persona." She picked up the pace and huffed and puffed as
she walked ahead.

"So homeschool, huh?" I said, trying to keep up. The dog
nipped at our heels. "Sounds awesome."

"I can't wait to get back to *school* school," she said. "Ever
hear of Beekman 26?"

"That's the arts school, right?"

"It's paradise. I'm there just as soon as I'm back to a hundred and eleven percent. That'll be the start of next quarter, definitely. Till then it's me and Dad at the kitchen table. A hundred and eleven's my favorite number, by the way. It's the atomic number of roentgenium. You can't find it in nature. You have to conjure it up in the lab, but it has the same properties as silver and gold. You probably knew that, being a sci-fi geek."

"A hundred and eleven's also the magic constant for the smallest magic square using the number one and prime numbers. Here, check it out." I grabbed her gel pen from behind her ear and wrote on my palm like this:

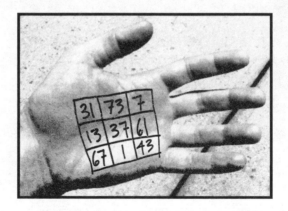

"Add those numbers vertically, horizontally or diagonally, and they equal a hundred and eleven," I said.

She grabbed my hand and added and nodded. "How do you know this?" she said. "You're like genius-level smart, aren't you? Like smart enough where I'll have to hate you for being smarter than me—than I am?"

"*No,*" I said. "You're totally smarter."

"All right then. In general, anyway. But clearly not in math. So annoying. I hate being a stereotype. You know, girl equals math dummy. Except I'm not. I was better than all the boys at school, if only to make them mad."

"I'm not mad."

"Why would you be? You don't go to my school."

"Huh?"

"Never mind, go on. I'm feeling better about you now, about our comparative intelligences. Please, continue."

"I got this book for Christmas once," I said. "It was like a math puzzle book." I held up my palm. "It's not like I thought this up myself or anything."

"Who said you did? Anyway, I'll need a copy of it." She pressed her palm on mine and the ink transferred to hers.

"It's backward," I said.

"It's perfect," she said. "My mom. She was right. You're cool. You've redeemed yourself, and from a *very* deep hole."

"Your dad. He's taking off work to be your tutor?"

"He works nights mostly. You're really twelve? You look older."

"Seriously? Thanks."

"You're hilarious."

"How much older?"

"Twelve and a half," she said.

"You're like thirteen, right?"

"Am. You're freaking hysterical."

"Why?"

"Oh my gosh, stop making me laugh."

"But you're not laughing."

"Do you have any money on you?" she said. "Buy me a Reese's and I'll forget that whole thing back at the library entirely."

"What, that I wanted to send your mom the wink?"

"Why are you reminding me?"

I bought a three-pack and we sat on a boardwalk bench. She nibbled the candy. "Sweet Cheez Whiz, that's good," she said. "This dog's very existence is preposterous. He's sho goofy I want to shmoosh him and munch him up into a biwwion widdiw peeshes of fwuff. Gonna eachou! How do you not have a name for this little freak? I love the way he looks at you."

"And how's that?"

"Constantly," she said. "You should get him certified as a therapy dog. That way he could come into the library, and nobody can give us dirty looks."

"You mean like a Seeing Eye dog?"

"Exactly not. Are you blind? There's this thing where kids who have a hard time reading, read to dogs. The dog doesn't judge the kid when he mispronounces a word or whatever. The dog's just completely psyched the kid is giving him all this attention. The kid feels like, whoa, this dog is totally listening to me, I must be reading pretty great. The more confident the kid gets, the better he reads. I swear, it's a real program. They do it in schools and libraries and jails and stuff. I think your little guy here could do it. Look at him listening to us. To me anyway. I talk a lot."

"Really?"

"Do you mean 'really' as in, do I think your guy could do it, or really I talk a lot?"

"That he could do it."

"Liar. Your eyes are open too wide and you're looking away." Any guy who thinks he's smarter than a girl is an idiot. But this girl was as smart as my mom, which was *totally* scary. "Read to Rufus, it's called, where the dog listens to the kid," she said. "I read about it in the education section of the paper. I'm going to be an English teacher by day and a novelist by night. You?"

I shrugged. "Waterslide tester?"

"That's the last thing I would've expected you or anybody to say. Okay, I am now officially falling in like with you. That is so freaking awesome. You are my hero." I think that's what she said. Things got fuzzy after *falling in like with you.* "Stop jackhammering your leg," she said. "It's spectacularly annoying."

"Sorry."

"Stop apologizing. Don't feel compelled to say anything at all. I know, I'm bossy."

"I'm not saying anything at all."

"Flip," she said. "That's what you should call him."

"Why?"

"Because that's his name. Watch. Flip. See? He cocked his head."

"He cocks it no matter what you say to him," I said.

"Flip Flip Flip Flip Flip."

The little dog licked the Rainbow Girl's lips and she smiled the most awesome smile, like in the picture of Mom's partner Laura. Not pushing it, just real. Then she pushed up from the bench and headed off. "Gotta go study. Dad's dropping an algebra test on me first thing tomorrow morning."

"Beats what I have, a quiz on chapters one through five of *To Kill a* freaking *Mockingbird*."

"What, you expect them to let you analyze *Starship Troopers* in English? At least you love *Feathers*, which means there's hope for you. Look into the therapy dog certification. Maybe I'll help you get that Read to Rufus thing going at the library. My mom would be totally into it."

We were backpedaling away from each other, and we had to shout now. "Hey, I'm sorry about your dog," I said.

"We're adopting a new one as soon as I'm a hundred and eleven percent."

"What's your name anyway?"

"Halley, like the comet."

"Wow."

"Yup."

"I'm, like, Ben, just so you know."

"I, like, know. Mom told me, plus it's on your library card, duh."

"What's it about, your novella?"

She spun around once and skipped and smiled. "I don't know you well enough to tell you yet!"

"Does that mean you'll be at the library tomorrow after school?"

"I have a doctor's appointment! We look like idiots, hollering as we're backing away from each other! You're about to backpedal into an old man in a wheelchair! Ben?"

"Yeah?"

"A hundred and eleven! That's how many books I'm going to write! That's how many years I'm going to live! Bye Flip!"

I texted Chucky.

> BC: Who told you the wink means profound admiration and respect?

> CM: Rayburn, why?

10

DESTINED FOR AMAZINGNESS

"He's going to be amazing with the kids," the lady at the Read to Rufus office said.

Mom elbowed me and got back to signing the paper that said she would sponsor my training to become a Read to Rufus facilitator because I was underage.

"This girl, my friend, we'd like to start a program at my library," I said.

"Sounds fantastic," the lady said. "You and Flip will need to attend some classes to get him certified. There's a bunch of homework too. Can you commit to that?"

"A hundred and eleven percent," I said.

"He's absolutely devoted to you, Ben," the lady said. "Go ahead, do it again. I'd like to take a picture and post it on the website, if you're cool with that."

I read to Flip from *The Memory Door*, by N. T. Castillo-Cormier. His little ears perked up and he cocked his head, his big gold eyes on me. When I winked at him he dove at my mouth and stuck his peanut-butter-stinking tongue in there.

"Check your training books about how to teach him not to fly at the reader's face," the lady said. Her phone camera clicked. "Keep going, Ben."

The book was about this guy who finds a doorway that'll let him travel a hundred and forty million years into the future. "'He opened the door and the whole Earth was ice. The sky was black even though the sun was shining. The sun itself was ten times bigger, but the future was all cold wind. He turned around to go back home, but the door had disappeared, and now it and everything and everyone he'd ever known and loved existed only in his memory.'"

The subway car was crowded on the way home. I left the backpack open, and Flip stuck his little head out to look around. This girl in the next seat said, "I want to cuddle him till I crush him." I held the backpack a little closer to me. The train stopped and the girl got off and actually said bye to me.

"Wield your newfound power gently, Traveler," Mom said. "Who's this friend you were talking about? The one who's going to help you set up a Read to Rufus clinic at the library?"

"You know, just this girl I met."

"Okay," Mom said. "How long have you known her?"

"Like, since last winter? Mom, she's a *library* girl, for cripe's sake. Relax."

She put me into a sort of headlock and kissed my forehead and then she went back to her book, some nonfiction thing about getting traumatized kids to talk again. That's what she did for work. That was how we met.

I didn't want to think about it anymore, the time before I went to live with Mom.

I put on my headphones and listened to the *Transformers* soundtrack and dreamed about the future, about all of us hanging out at the library: Flip and me and the Read to Rufus kids and Halley Like the Comet.

11
I WRITE,
THEREFORE I AM

Wednesday was Rayburn-free. Word was getting around
school that he cut out to do something illegal, not to mention profitable. Angelina started the rumor, and the way she
said it, I was pretty sure she thought Rayburn was the most
fascinating humanoid on the planet. "He's gonna be so rich
someday!" Big deal. A rich moron, some prize.

Chucky and I were going to eat in the cafeteria, but the
urge for half-decent slices overwhelmed us and we went out
to Nice Guy Eddie's. "Does she have a nice butt at least, the
library chick?"

"Mold?"

"*Coffin?*"

"Do I need to smack the snot out of you?"

"Sure, pick on the short kid. *Now* you're a tough guy. My
hero. Are you going to eat the rest of that?"

"What, you want to lick the plate?" I said. He did, too.

After school I picked up Flip and we went to the library. I looked through the window and saw the place was packed. Somebody was bound to hiss, "No dogs allowed!" I rapped on the glass until Mrs. Lorentz came out.

"I did what Halley said. I started getting Flip certified as a therapy dog."

"Totally awesome," Mrs. Lorentz said. "Coincidentally, she started looking into setting up the reading clinic here. She was just talking about you, in fact. She said, 'I bet sci-fi boy shows up in ten minutes.' That was—"

"Ten minutes ago," Halley said as she came outside. She wore a red beret and a black hoodie with white writing on the front that said: I WRITE, THEREFORE I AM. She scooped up Flip and slung her backpack over her shoulder. "Let's go."

"Where?"

"You know on the back wall inside, the picture *Dreamland at Night*?" she said.

"It's my favorite."

"It's everybody's." She grabbed my hand and led me toward the water.

I'd never held hands with anybody before, especially in front of their mom.

"I'm not crushing on you," she said.

"No, I know," I said. "Just friends, totally."

"*Just*? What's better than friends? Sorry my hands are freezing."

"I don't mind," I said.

She double squeezed my hand and we didn't say anything for a while and just walked sort of fast. We both breathed hard. Then she said, "So?"

"So."

"What's your dad do?"

"Who knows?" I said.

"Oh," she said. "Sorry."

I shrugged. "My mom's a speech pathologist, though."

"That's awesome."

"What's your dad do?" I said.

"He's a magician. What's with the face?"

"No, that's cool."

"It *is*, at least that's what everybody says except you."

"They're sneaky," I said. "Their purpose in life is to trick you."

"To make you *believe*," she said.

"In what?"

"A hundred and eleven." She showed me her palm. She'd retraced the backward imprint from Monday with a sparkly purple marker.

"The magic box," she said.

The magic box. I blinked it away. "It's actually called a magic square," I said. "Besides, that's math, not magic."

"They're the same thing," she said.

"I kind of had a bad experience with a magician this one time." I blinked harder to push it back.

"Tell me," she said.

"What's your book about?" I said.

She rolled her eyes. "Okay, I'll show you."

We went to the new Luna Park. It was closed that day, but we looked through the fence. The golden tower from 1905 was gone. Flip begged me to pick him up. This seagull was giving him bad eyes, like he'd make a nice snack. The roller-coaster track was one of those high-tech ones, just one long mean rail slicing up the gray sky. "I like the old one better," I said.

"I love 'em both," Halley said.

"The 1905 one was all silvery and soft gold."

"Because it's a black-and-white *picture*, hello? The new one's *bright*. Look at all that pink paint. Anyway, you'd be able to go back and visit the old one if I let you read my novella. Which of course I totally won't, not ever, which is a shame since the most pivotal scene in the whole entire story is set in Luna Park, 1905."

"I understand. I won't push you—"

"Okay, *okay* already, if you insist. But for all my bravado

I'm actually spectacularly fragile when it comes to my art, so even if you hate it, tell me you love it. I'm perfectly okay with being lied to on that score."

"Deal."

She huffed. "So there's this girl."

"There always is," I said.

"She runs away to Luna Park."

"The new one or the old one?"

"Both."

"Interesting," I said. "Why's she run away? Crummy parents?"

"They died instantly in a car crash."

"They always do."

"Well, you have to get rid of them somehow, and that seemed the most merciful yet expeditious way. Otherwise how do you turn her into an orphan? This is a middle grade story, like for ages ten to fourteen, and the rule is you need an orphan."

"I hear you."

"The girl, she has these flying dreams all the time. She thinks they mean she's supposed to be a trapeze artist, so she starts training to do that. You know the ride where you can do the trapeze, and you're connected to safety cables in case you fall? Well, she's the one who hooks you up to the wires."

"The ride attendant."

"At night, when the park closes, she practices. Problem is,

she's not very good. She doesn't have the confidence, you know? She needs somebody to cheer her on."

"This is where the boy comes in. Let me guess: He's the guy who keeps the lights on for her after the park shuts down. The park electrician or whatever, right?"

"No, but I like that. I may steal it."

"All yours. Everybody's always stealing from me anyway."

"What do they steal?" she said. "Are you rich? I'm both suspicious of and fascinated by rich people."

"For a twelve-year-old I do okay. I have probably like the third-biggest coupon delivery route in my whole district."

"Golly."

"Thanks. Yeah. So how do they meet in the first place, the girl and the boy?"

"Through the girl's friend, this magician who works at the park," she said, "and I'm going to stop right there for now. You'll have to meet my dad before I can continue."

"Why?"

"Because you have to believe in magic for this story to work, and Mercurious Raines is the best person to get you there."

"Mercurious *Raines?*"

"Yup. Okay, so from what you've heard so far, the setup, what do you think?"

"I love it."

"You're lying again." She pecked my cheek and grabbed Flip and they went down to the water. She cheered Flip on as he chased the wave froth. The sun came through here and there and it was like spotlights. One of them passed over Halley and she was gold for around ten or eleven seconds.

All I could think about on the way home was that I didn't want to move to Florida now. Flip started whimpering as we came to my apartment building, probably because the rain was starting, I figured. Nope.

I stepped into the apartment and saw an old lady sitting at the kitchen table with Mom. Flip jumped into the woman's lap. She smothered him with kisses and said, "Darling, how Mommy missed you!"

12

THE TRAVELER
FROM THE PAST

Flip licked the tears out of the old lady's eyes. Her clothes were dirty, her sneakers worn thin. She showed me a grimy picture, her and Flip all cuddled up in front of a pine tree lit silver and red. In the picture the woman looked nice, pretty clothes, sweet smile. The dog's tail wasn't bent and chomped. It was all fluffed up like somebody went at it with a blow dryer for an hour and a half. "Spencer's first Christmas," she said.

"We've been calling him Flip," I said. When the dog heard the name Halley gave him he squirmed out of the woman's arms and hopped up into my lap. He was shivering.

"Where do you live?" Mom said. She poured the woman coffee.

The woman called out, "*Spen*cer. Here now, my angel."

I set him down. He hesitated. He went to her, licked her hand once and came right back to me.

The woman nodded. "I see," she said. She looked around our nice comfy kitchen. She stopped on the picture of Laura. She looked at Flip in my arms. "Spencer seems to have found a fine, safe home here," the woman said. "Flip, I mean. He seems to have found himself a family."

I wasn't going to say anything to that, but Mom was halfway into "Well, now, let's talk about this," when the woman just up and ran out of our apartment.

"Ben, get the umbrella and come with me," Mom said. "Leave Flip here."

The elevator doors closed just as we got to them. By the time the next one came and we got to the lobby, the woman was gone. We went outside. Here it was September, and the air was cold with all the rain. It tore the leaves from the trees. Then I saw her at the end of the street, sitting on the curb.

"Come back inside," Mom said. "We'll have some nice hot soup."

"Forty dollars," the woman said. "I got sick and had to go into the hospital. I couldn't pay my doctor's bills. I lost my apartment. They don't let animals into the homeless shelters. We slept in the waiting rooms at the airport terminals, traipsing from one to the other when the security guards made us move. When I fell asleep, a man tried to take Spencer. After that we slept in the ATM lobbies. I was begging out in front of the bank one night, holding the door for people on their way to the cash machine. A woman said she would give me forty dollars for Spencer. She seemed like a nice woman. I thought Spencer would be safer with her."

"You were going to sell him again, if we gave him to you just now, right?" I said.

"Ben," Mom said. "I won't have you talking that way to our fellow traveler."

"She's not my fellow anything."

"I could never do that to him again," the old woman said. "I still can't believe I did it. I couldn't feed him anymore. I couldn't feed *me*. I was starving."

"Do you see how messed up his tail is?"

"Not another word, son," Mom said. "Come with us," she said to the lady. "I can help you find the help you need."

"What I need is money."

Mom took all the money out of her wallet and gave it to the woman. "Ben, give our friend here whatever you have."

I reached into my pocket. "I only have a dollar," I lied. All year round I delivered those coupons before school, rain, sleet, heat, snow. In winter I shoveled sidewalks and driveways on the block where the people owned one-family houses. In summer I washed their cars and weeded their gardens. First Rayburn and now this lady. Why should I hand over my money to somebody who sold Flip to a stranger? I was so mad I didn't even want to let her have the crumpled dollar.

"Give it to her," Mom said.

I put the bill into the woman's hand, and she took off.

Mom nudged me to follow her. "Here, go, give her the umbrella."

The lady wouldn't take it. She kept going.

"Thank you, Ben," Mom said.

"It was just a stupid dollar."

"It was everything."

That night Flip did great at his training session for the therapy dog certification. He already knew lots of tricks, roll over and play dead and even this one called the fighter. The guy running the class said, "Flip, box." That little dog stood on his hind legs and jabbed the air with his front paws. I couldn't stop thinking about the old lady and how many hours she must have spent teaching him that one.

It took a long time to get home. The rain made the trains run slow. Mom nudged me. "Cheer up."

I took Flip out of the backpack and he snored in my lap and I cheered up.

13

THE UNEXPECTED
SOLUTION TO THE
FLORIDA PROBLEM

Thursday was good all through school because Rayburn was "out sick" again. On the way home Mold wanted me to come over and chill for a round or two of *Infinite Crisis*, but Flip and I had a date with Halley, except it wasn't a date. "She's a *friend*," I said.

"That's not what I asked," Chucky said. He'd asked if she was a babe.

"She's beautiful," I said.

Chucky rolled his eyes. "Compared to Mystique from X-Men, *beautiful* like that?"

"There's no comparison. Mystique is completely blue and this girl's a rainbow."

"Mystique is also completely naked," Chucky said. "A

rainbow, huh? Dude, the way you talk sometimes? You're a riddle wrapped inside an enchilada."

"Enigma."

"See, like right there. Quit looking so bummed out." We were at the corner where we usually split up, but I guess Chucky could tell I needed to talk, because he went with me up the block, toward my building. Turns out he should've just gone home.

"I'm setting up this whole Read to Rufus thing, and in nine months I'm out of here."

"So you set up another one in Florida," Chucky said. "Of course the *rain*bow babe won't be in Florida, but there's still tons of chicks down there." He slugged my shoulder. "Ow," he said. "Bony shoulder you got there. Ow," he said again.

Rayburn had just slapped him in the back of the head. "Pockets," he said. Angelina giggled and Ronda just looked mean.

Chucky turned his pockets inside out: nothing but an empty Skittles wrapper.

"Let's go, Coffin," Rayburn said.

"No," I said.

"What?" Rayburn said.

"What?" Chucky said.

"*What?*" Angelina said.

"Coffin, don't be mental," Ronda said.

Rayburn shoved me, but I stayed on my feet. "No," I said.

"Good for you, Ben," Chucky said.

"Shut up, Mold." Rayburn cracked him across the mouth. I shoved Rayburn and then everybody went nuts. Rayburn was belting me and Angelina was kicking Chucky and Ronda was yelling for everybody to stop being mental and shoving everybody in sight. Half a minute later they were gone and my pockets were empty. The idiot took my headphones too.

I don't know how long it was before I could breathe anywhere near normal. I was on my back, looking up. The pigeons were looking down at me from where they hung out under the elevated train tracks and pooped on everybody. Chucky kept asking me if I was okay, I think. I had a hard time understanding him because his lip was stuck to his braces. We huddled behind the dumpster—always dumpsters for us—and got ourselves together. "Do I need stitches?" Chucky said.

"No, it's just a fat lip. Quit crying," I said. "Quit it!"

I wiped the blood from my nose and turned my sweatshirt inside out to hide the rest of it. No way was I telling Mom. She'd be on the phone with Mrs. Pinto before the words were out of my mouth, and things would be ten times worse in school. I'd explain away the fat eye with the old gym excuse, "I got nailed in dodge ball."

When I got home Flip wasn't at the door waiting for me. "Flip? C'mon bud, let's go see Halley."

He crawled out of Mom's room real fast to my feet. I picked him up and boy was he trembling.

This old lady was in my mother's room, facedown on the floor. It took me a few seconds before I figured out who it was, even though she wasn't supposed to be home from work for another two hours. "Mom?"

She was cold the way you can't be when you're alive. It looked like she died in the middle of putting on her sneakers. That was the other reason we were moving to Florida—her health. Her heart acted a little fluttery in the New York winter, she said.

The weirdest thing? I was kind of mad at her. What the heck was I supposed to do now?

14
ITCHY SOCKS

The next four days passed in a blur. I didn't sleep, didn't have one asthma attack, didn't cry one tear. I was actually kind of mellow. It's not like any of this was a surprise. Here was the proof: Nothing perfect lasts forever.

I do remember one thing very clearly, breakfast the first day of the wake. I was making myself some Cap'n Crunch when Aunt Jeanie came in and said, "That's not a proper breakfast, Ben. That's not even food. Let me make you something that's—oh!" She clutched her chest, like she was about to follow in Mom's footsteps. "Your slacks!"

They were a little short. I must have grown another inch in the last year, since the last time I wore them to my interview for my coupon delivery job, which everybody laughed at me for—but hey, I got the job. "You can see your socks!"

"Only a little," I said, lowering my pants some, except they were already below where my butt crack started.

"They're white!"

"So?" That's what Mom would have said. "So they see your socks, Ben? Is the world going to stop spinning? You look cool. In fact, I might wear my slacks like that too." And she would have hiked them right up and laughed. Aunt Jeanie, on the other hand, turned into a freakazoid. "Let's go," she said. "In the car. Now." The whole way over to Macy's she kept saying, "This is a disaster. You poor dear. If Tess could see us now, she'd have my head on a platter."

Really, she would have said, *Jeanie? Take a pill.*

"We'll get you fixed right up, don't you worry at all."

"I'm really not worried, though," I said.

"You poor thing." She called ahead for them to have a pair of slacks ready for us. She was like the queen when we walked in there. The sales assistant practically bowed to her. She waved him off and said, "Abso*lute*ly not," when the guy suggested a pair of pants that were only half lame, sort of comfy-looking like jeans but with dress pants material, very shiny. "We're not going out to a *night*club, Angelo. We're going to my big sister's . . ." She got all teary.

"Jeanie, I'm so sorry," Angelo said, or would have said if Aunt Jeanie didn't cut him off.

"This young man has a classic look. No no, here." She grabbed a pair of the thoroughly lamest pants in all of Macy's, the kind you see in the catalog where the models are all old men who would have like these tufts of frizzly gray hair growing out of their ears if they didn't trim it.

"Perfect," she said. "Hurry, Ben, go put them on while I get you some proper socks." I swear she picked the itchiest pair in the store.

By Sunday night all the people I never met till now but who hugged me like they knew me forever were gone, and it was just Aunt Jeanie, Leo, me and Flip at the kitchen table. Aunt Jeanie kept at it with the face cream but she couldn't hide the fact she'd been crying pretty much the whole way through the past four days. I heard her at night, through the wall. She and Leo were camped out in Mom's room. "Don't let the dog sit in your lap like that, Ben," Jeanie said. "Not in those nice slacks. The fur. You'll never get it out."

"Babe, easy," Leo said. "You want to end up like your sister?"

"Nice, Leo," she said.

"Ah honey, I'm sorry," he said.

"*Nice.*"

"You know what I mean."

I put Flip on the floor between my feet. He sat like he'd learned at the training place, front paws up, like give me high ten, and that's when I realized I missed his last certification class. I had one chance to make it up, or else we had to start all over and pay the whole fee again too.

"So we have to talk about how things will go from here," Aunt Jeanie said. "Clearly you'll come live with us. Tess left directions, and that's what she wanted. She put away some money for you too, enough to get you through the first two years of college, maybe. She left me in charge of the money until you turn eighteen."

I already knew this stuff. Mom told me and asked if I'd be okay with what she had in mind for me in case she died. I was like, "Sure." What choice did I have?

"Look, champ, it's all going to be okay," Leo said. "I'm even excited about this in a weird way. Not in a weird way. You know what I mean. I can be your coach in Little League or something."

Leo was huge, but a lot of that was fat. I couldn't see him throwing a ball without having a stroke. He was probably sixty-something but looked older. "I don't want to be a problem," I said.

"Stop talking like that," Aunt Jeanie said. "We're happy to have you."

"Happy to have you," Leo said too, almost, but Aunt Jeanie cut him off.

"The first order of business is to take whatever you want from the apartment. I have to return the keys to the landlord by the end of the month, and I'm having somebody come in to sell the furniture and such. Whatever you don't want, goes."

"Champ, there's not a lot of room at the house. All those books. You might want to consider thinning out the collection there. I'm gonna get you the e-book versions, much more efficient."

"It's okay," I said.

"No no, I want to do it," Leo said. "I want to buy you a present, okay? I feel bad for you, being orphaned again and all that."

"Leo, really?" Aunt Jeanie said.

"No, I'm just saying," Leo said.

"I can sell them back to Strand," I said. "The used bookstore. That's where a lot of them came from anyway."

"There you go," Leo said. "Put a few dollars in your pocket. Very enterprising, my kind of guy."

I looked around the apartment. My eyes settled on the picture of Laura. "Can I bring her?"

"Well, now, that will be fine, Ben," Aunt Jeanie said. She patted my shoulder from a distance, leaning away as she reached in. "Yes, I suspect Tess would want that."

Tess. Not Mom. Two years I knew her. I got kind of mad all of a sudden. It hit me: That was the longest I ever knew anybody. I excused myself, and Flip and I went to my room, which was about to be somebody else's soon. I pulled down my Chewbacca poster, rolled it up and slipped it into a tube of gift-wrapping paper that said CONGRATULATIONS! again and again.

I checked my phone. I had like a dozen texts from Halley. They started Thursday afternoon with *Where are you?* and ended Saturday morning with *I have no idea what I did to make you blow me off, but whatever it is I'm sorry.*

I just didn't know how to get back to her. What, I'm going to tell her my mom died when I barely know her? I don't know, I just didn't want her feeling bad for me or bad at all, even though I knew I was making her feel bad not getting back to her.

"Ben?"

I practically jumped off the bed when Aunt Jeanie came in. Mom always knocked, even if the door was open, which it wasn't.

"Your principal left messages for Tess. Three. Apparently you've been fighting?"

I knew freaking Chucky would cave.

15

NO SMOKING IN MRS. PINTO'S

The next day after school we had a big meeting in Mrs. Pinto's office: Rayburn and his mom, Angelina and Ronda and theirs, Chucky and Mrs. Mold, and me and Leo, because Aunt Jeanie had to work. Turns out it wasn't Chucky who ratted out Rayburn. It was Ronda.

Rayburn's mom put one of those electronic cigarette things to her lips.

"Uh, excuse me, *no*," Mrs. Pinto said.

"It's not real smoke," Rayburn's mom said. "It's *water*."

"It's not happening anywhere near school property," Mrs. Pinto said. "Okay, so Damon, you have something for Ben."

He gave me the headphones. I didn't even want them now that he'd worn them.

"And?"

Rayburn rolled his eyes. His mom yelled, "Damon, you want to get locked up? Shake those boys' hands. *Mean* it too."

He was shaking as he shook our hands. He was this close to killing somebody or crying. Angelina was huffing and Ronda rolled her eyes.

"Now *sign* that contract," his mom said. It said he promised to meet with the guidance counselor twice a week. He signed.

"That's it?" Chucky said. "He's not going to jail? Not even a freaking *suspension*? He punched me in the mouth!"

"Charles," Mrs. Mold said.

"I kind of have to agree with Chuck here," Leo said. "Look, I'm not saying we gotta hook Dennis to the ball and chain—boys will be boys and all—but don't you think he's getting off a little light? I mean, going to the *guidance* counselor? Do we really think that's going to work?"

"And what do you want *Damon* to do instead?" Rayburn's mom said, like she was ready to stick her non-smoky cigarette into Leo's eye.

"Let Chuck smack him back?" Leo said. "Hey, relax, I was just *kidding.*"

Everybody stared at Leo.

Mrs. Pinto sent us kids out while she talked to the parents and Leo. Rayburn and Angelina stormed off, glaring at me like everything was my fault.

"Thanks," I said to Ronda.

"I only did it because your mom died," she said. "You're still not allowed to say hi to me in the hall." She gave me a halfhearted shove and went off the other way. I plunked down on the bench outside Mrs. Pinto's office. Chucky plunked next to me. "Me too, Coffin," he said. "Sorry about your mom." He put his arm over my shoulder, but I shrugged it off. "I'm *fine*, Mold, okay? Seriously."

"Okay," he said. Chucky's fingertip traced what somebody scratched into the bench: THE OTHER WAY TO SPELL FAILURE? Y-O-U.

When we got home, or what used to be home, Flip was already by the door with one of my dirty socks and my collector's edition Wolverine action figure. Leo almost tripped over Flip. "We might have to start making him wear a blinking light," he said. "I've seen rats bigger than him. I guess we better get you packed up now, champ."

"I'm ready." I nodded to where I'd put a bag of clothes and a box of books with the picture of Laura and my Chewie poster.

"That's it?" Leo said.

I'd already packed the other books and brought the boxes down to the mailroom that morning.

Leo clapped my shoulder. "Jeanie won't be back from work till eight. Let's play a video game or something. I'll order a couple of pizzas."

"I have to walk Flip," I said.

"When you get back."

"Actually, I have to meet a friend."

"Gotcha," he said.

"What time do you want me home for dinner?"

"I mean, whenever Tess used to say, I guess, right?"

16
THE EXPLODED RAINBOW

Mrs. Lorentz wasn't at the front desk, so that was good at least. Halley's notebooks and sparkle pens were spread all over the table like an exploded rainbow. Black beret today. Glaring green eyes for just a second and then no time for me. "This is me not talking to you," she said.

"I'm sorry."

"You're an idiot."

"I know."

"You don't know anything. My mother and I were like, did he die or something? Gimme your freaking backpack." She scooped Flip into her lap. "Here I'm doing all this research about the Read to Rufus stuff. Me and Mom are on a video conference with this school where the kids have a hard time reading. Everybody's completely psyched, and we're telling them we're ready as soon as you and Flip are, and you like vanish? What the freak? What did I do? Where were you? And what happened to your face?"

I told her, and then I told her everything else. You know how you can tell when somebody's really listening to you? Like you can almost see the words traveling through the air, into her eyes, and then they sink into her heart? Like she wants to take in the way you feel, even if you're sad, because she wants to be there with you? For you? She hugged me and whispered, "It's okay, it's okay, you can cry."

"I'm really okay," I whispered back.

"No, really, you can. I want you to."

"But I don't want to."

She leaned back a little to look at me. She looked at me for a while, and then she tilted her head to the side. I swear it was like I went from hardly knowing her to knowing her better than I ever knew anybody, maybe even Mom. No, the other way around. She knew me. She could read my mind. "You feel like you can't breathe, right?" she said. "Let's get out of here."

That afternoon was crazy warm for September, and the boardwalk was busy. Somehow her hand was even colder today. "Cypress Hills, by the cemeteries?" she said. That's where Jeanie and Leo lived. "Are you changing schools?"

"No, I'm not being the new kid again." Everybody kept stopping to pet Flip, and he loved it.

"How long were you in there?" she said.

"Where?"

"Foster care."

"Until like two years ago."

She stopped walking. "Why'd it take so long?"

"I was a drop-off," I said. "At the police station, you know? A few days old, my file says. They do blood tests on you, to see if you're healthy. My blood had drugs in it."

"From your mom."

"That scares people away." I shrugged. "The only thing I'm addicted to is those chocolate chip cookies your mom leaves out on her desk."

"Ben? I'm sorry."

"Why? The caretakers were cool, most always." I held back on the fact that everything was always changing. People coming and going. You'd make a friend one day and she'd be gone the next or maybe you would be. After a while you stopped trying to remember names. "One Christmas we had a grab bag. I ended up with this Chewbacca poster. I never hung it. I figured I'd only have to take it down again." I was doing it again, saying what I was thinking. "Hey, did you tell your dad I hate magic?"

"He said he'd like to show you a trick or two."

"I don't think so," I said.

"You can tell me, you know? About your mom?"

"I did."

"You told me she died. You didn't tell me about *her*."

"She's in a better place and all that, right?" I said. "Nothing to be sad about, Traveler."

"Traveler?"

"Life's a journey. The best part is going uphill. Things come all at once, bad brings good, one door closes, two open, go through both."

"She used to say that to you, right?"

"Really, Halley, I'm okay. Yeah. It's windy." I said that in case I started to cry, which I didn't.

"It *is* windy."

"I wish we had sunglasses," I said.

"Yeah." She squeezed my hand really hard and didn't let go and we kept walking fast and didn't look at each other or say anything for a while.

"Like, how are *you* feeling?" I said.

"Shut up, Ben."

"I'm sorry."

"No, it's just, I don't know, your mom dies, and you're worried about me?"

"No, not worried—totally not. Just seeing if, like, you're feeling good. You know."

"Don't worry about me. I don't like to lose."

"I know."

"You better. My good numbers are up, the bad numbers are down. I'm awesome. So are you. Flip's more awesome than both of us. We are a trio of terrificness. Yeah." Suddenly she pulled me off the boardwalk toward the street. "Frick it," she said. "It's time for you to meet the one and only Mercurious Raines. C'mon Flip!"

17

THE LABORATORY OF MERCURIOUS RAINES

He rented office space in a church basement. The entrance was a red door with black metal hinges. Gothic letters spelled out:

THE LABORATORY OF MERCURIOUS RAINES
ENTER AT YOUR OWN RISK . . .

(MAGIC LESSONS BY APPOINTMENT)

"You've really never heard of him?" Halley said. "He's like the king of the bar mitzvah circuit. He does stuff in Manhattan too." She pushed on the door and it *creeeeaked*. Flip pawed at my leg to be picked up.

The music was blaring, *Fantasia, The Sorcerer's Apprentice*. The walls were like the ones at the library, silkscreened with giant pictures. There were Saturn and the moon, and then the Halo Galaxy, and burning bright across the ceiling, Halley's Comet.

A few parents watched from the back. Three little kids

sat in folding chairs and watched a fourth learn a trick from a man in a sparkly purple sweat suit and a white cape. He looked maybe forty. He wore a silver sombrero. His hair was long and pulled back in a ponytail. His goatee was a little long too. Mercurious Raines wore gold basketball sneakers that were so shiny I felt like I was looking into the sun. He knelt on one knee next to the kid onstage and patted the kid's back.

"Go ahead," he said.

The kid frowned. He snapped his fingers, and a world globe the size of a basketball materialized, spinning on his fingertip. "No way," the kid said. "I did that?"

"*You* did," Mercurious Raines said.

"I *did* it, Mom," the kid said.

Halley elbowed me.

"You have sharp elbows," I whispered.

"You have fantastically sensitive ribs," she said.

After the class Halley introduced me and Flip to her dad. "Not a big magic fan, I hear, Ben?"

"How'd you do that thing with the globe?" I said. "Or is this one of those 'A great magician never reveals his secrets'?"

"Oh, I think a true magician shares all the magic he can," he said. "Give me a minute to make a phone call, and then I'll show you the globe illusion." He stepped into a smaller room where he had his desk and closed the door most of the way.

"See?" Halley said. "He's not some evil warlock, right?"

"He's nice."

"Halley, Ben, can you guys help me for a sec?" Mr. Lorentz called from behind his office door. "I can't find my phone. I swear, if my head wasn't attached to my shoulders, I'd lose that too."

I pushed through the door. Mr. Lorentz was standing on the far side of the room, or most of him was. His head was gone.

It was on the other side of the room, on his desk. It said, "Oh wait, there it is." And then back on the far side of the room, his headless body pulled the phone from his back pocket. The headless body crossed to the desk and held the phone to Mr. Lorentz's bodiless head. The head said to the body, "Would you mind dialing for me?"

Halley was cracking up and Flip sprinted circles around the headless body. I pulled out my inhaler and sucked in a double shot.

The headless body stepped toward me, and Mr. Lorentz's head was back on his shoulders. "Ben, it's just mirrors and video projection, son," he said.

"No, I know, it's just I have to get home for dinner." I scooped up Flip and got out of there. I didn't get more than a block away before I had to sit on the steps of an apartment building. Flip nudged my hand to pet him.

Halley showed up out of breath. "Okay, need I remind you I finished a round of chemotherapy not long ago? A little getting out and about and moving around is good for me, but I'm not ready for an all-out sprint. You're actually not as slow as I thought you'd be."

"I truly appreciate that."

She rubbed my back and after a while we'd caught our breath. "Let's have it," she said. "Where's the magician trauma come from?"

"Tell me about your novella. What happens next?"

"I'll tell you after you tell me. Clearly this is something awesome we have shaping up here, this friendship. We click." She winked at me. "So?"

So I told it to her, the story of the magic box.

18
THE MAGIC BOX

Kayla was her name. She was five, I was almost ten. She was my shadow. I was the oldest in the group home and I read to the little kids a lot. She had asthma too. We'd be in the kitchen together, on the nebulizers. They're these machines that help you breathe better. Lots of kids had asthma in that neighborhood. We were just downwind of the power plant.

Anyway, this one time, between puffs of medicine, Kayla and I were gabbing away, which you're not supposed to do when you're hooked up to the machine, but Kayla was all psyched because Christmas was coming. Santa appeared to her in a dream and said he was bringing her a box filled with magic. I was like, "What kind of magic?"

"The real kind," she said. "He told me it's the greatest treasure."

So I already had the box, this old wooden jewelry case I found on the street on garbage night, which is where I found a lot of my books too. This box was perfect, Halley,

I swear—dark blue velvet inside. So what if the top was a little cracked? I could glue it back together, right? But I was like totally freaked for the next two weeks, trying to figure out what I was going to put in that box. I mean, what can be the greatest treasure? The only thing you'll ever need to be happy? It doesn't exist.

Then, two days before Christmas, I figured it out, and of course it was a book. *The Little Prince.* That was the book that got me into sci-fi, this kid flying around the solar system, trying to find out what makes life so beautiful, right? And you learn that your eyes aren't really the things that let you see. That you can only truly see with your heart. Anyway, I figured it was as close as I could get to real magic, reading that book to Kayla. So my foster caregiver took me to the bookstore. I had just enough allowance saved up to get the book, and it fit perfectly in the box.

Christmas Eve came. Every year we had a Santa, and this time it was a Santa magician, and he was flat-out terrific. I mean he turned candle smoke into a goblin head. He made coins spark and vanish and reappear in the kids' hands. I was beginning to think this guy was for real, that magic was real. I was beginning to believe. Then he made a book flap its covers and flutter like a dove, and that's when I got the idea that maybe he could do the same thing with *The Little Prince*, so Kayla really would think it was the greatest treasure.

All the kids were oohing and ahhing, except I was beginning to get the idea Magic Santa kind of didn't want to be with us, a bunch of rejects, because he kept looking at his watch. Pretty soon he was rushing through the show, one trick into the next, no break for applause. He made me his assistant, simple stuff, hold this, get me that. I was standing next to him the whole time, and his phone kept buzzing. Finally he said he had to step out for a sec, Mrs. Claus was calling, he'd be right back.

Our caretaker could tell the guy was stressed, and she told me to bring him a cup of hot cider. So I did, and he's in this huge fight with his girlfriend, practically yelling into the phone, "What do you want me to do? It's a hundred bucks. I just have to give them the stupid presents, then I'm out of here." Then it was, "Fine, good, spend Christmas by yourself." He stuffed the phone into his pocket and noticed me. He sighed. "Sorry you heard that. Let's get back in there and finish up."

"Can I ask you a favor?" I said, and then I asked him if he could make *The Little Prince* fly.

"No way," he said. He told me the other book wasn't really a book at all but a bunch of cardboard rigged special with super-thin wires.

I was a little heartbroken, I have to admit. It made me realize everything else he did was fake too. I mean, that awesome trick with the coins? Who doesn't want to believe things can vanish and then come back? "It all looked so real," I said.

He rolled his eyes. "Why do you need the book to fly?" he said.

So I told him about Kayla and the magic box and how she's expecting this thing inside it to be a surprise that takes your breath away. Those were the exact words I used too. He repeated them, "A surprise that takes your breath away. Okay," he said. "I'll make it a big deal. She'll flip."

"What are you going to do?" I said.

"Just trust me," he said. "It'll leave her breathless."

So I went back in and rounded up the kids for the grab bag. Everybody got something they loved, except Kayla. You could tell she was about to cry, until Magic Santa said, "Now wait, I almost forgot, I have one last present here, a most special present, a magic box for Kayla." He reached under his big red cape and presented it like with a flourish, you know? Kayla was so flipped out her eyes went from almonds to circles. He held the box in front of her and told her to lift the lid, and before she did, she said, "See Ben? Magic is real."

She lifted the lid and this burst of crackly red smoke shot out, all the way up to the ceiling, in like half a second. Everybody jumped back, but then we're clapping, because it was such a cool surprise, right? And we're all covered in this red glitter. And then everybody stopped clapping.

Kayla was on the floor. She rolled up like a pill bug, and she was breathless all right. She couldn't breathe. Everybody was yelling call the ambulance, she has asthma, and the magician was like, "But it's not real smoke. It's just glitter. It's harmless."

But it was the fright that triggered the attack, and it was a really bad one. She was so shocked and panicked her throat started to close up. I was trying to make her breathe off of my inhaler, but she couldn't do it. The nebulizer was no good either. By the time the paramedics got there her chest was all puffed up because she couldn't get the air out of her lungs, and she's passing out and there's this shriek. Her wheezing. Like somebody's screaming, far away. Like you can't see them but you know they're being murdered.

19
FIRE ALARMS AND FIRE ESCAPES

"She died?" Halley said.

"No, I did," I said. "To her anyway. They took her to the hospital. They let me visit her once, and then the next day she was moved to this special unit, and you had to be family to get in, except nobody believed me when I said I was her family. She was in there for a week, and then of course a new kid came to take her spot in the house, and they moved her to a new home, they said. They couldn't tell me where, of course, her being a minor and all. They keep all that stuff private until you're sixteen. I wrote her letters. My caretaker promised she sent them, but I never heard back."

Halley traced the backward numbers written into her palm. The ink was fading, and pretty soon none of it would add up to a hundred and eleven. She frowned and nodded. "I'm doing the time line in my head. You were almost ten, you said, when Kayla—when this happened. You must have been adopted pretty much right after."

"I couldn't talk from the minute I found out Kayla wasn't coming back to the house. I don't know why. I mean, I was always really quiet, but after that I just forgot how to do it. To make the sounds. I knew what I wanted to say, but I couldn't get the words from my brain to my mouth. They sent Mom in to help me."

"How'd she do it?" Halley said. "How'd she get you speaking again?"

"She visited me three times a week. She'd ask me how I was doing today, and I'd try to talk, and nothing would happen, so I'd just nod my head. She didn't push me. She told me to tap it into her laptop, what I wanted to say. She asked me, 'What do you like?' and I typed *books*. 'Which ones?' *Science fiction mostly*. 'Have you ever read *Dune*?' *That's one of my favorites*. 'Mine too,' and we'd go back and forth like that. She'd bring in the books and read to me for a little bit. She had this awesome voice, like totally calm. There was a fire alarm drill, and everybody was all like, line up, hurry, eyes front, no talking, *march*, and meanwhile Mom whispers to me, 'This is a good time for you and me to sneak out to Dunkin' Donuts.'

"So maybe about the third week, I tapped into her iPad that I couldn't figure out where the words were getting stuck. I had this feeling that if she could show me where in my brain they were gunking up, like maybe show me on a picture or something, I could push them through. I just didn't know where to push. And then she does this thing. It was *true* magic, no offense to your dad. She puts her hand on my head and says, 'I'm so glad you told me this, Ben. We're home free. The words aren't stuck here.' She taps my forehead. 'They're stuck *here*.' Now she rests her hand on my heart. 'Oh,' I said. That was it. She didn't go crazy or anything, like screaming about the fact she got me to talk. She just messed up my hair a little and said, 'So why don't you tell me about Kayla?' And I did. Look, I know it wasn't totally my fault, okay?"

"Who, Kayla? It wasn't at all. *The Little Prince.* That was so awesome. It wasn't the Santa dude's fault either. I know you know that too."

"I guess," I said. "No, I know. He was flipping out."

"I bet," Halley said. "Poor guy."

Flip nudged Halley's hand and then did his boxer trick. Halley smiled and kissed him but she wasn't ready to stop being sad yet, which is why I didn't want to tell her the story in the first place.

"Thanks," I said. "There's only one other person I can talk to like this. Could talk to."

"She's still with you," Halley said.

"Sure."

"She is. She'll always be with you. Kayla too."

"Tell me the rest of your book."

"Not now," she said.

"When?"

"Soon."

"I've really been wanting to ask you about it. What kind it is. I just don't know how."

"You just did," she said.

"No, your, you know."

"Cancer? It isn't mine."

I nodded, feeling like a jerk.

"I want to tell you about it," she said. "I will, okay? I know it's not fair, you telling me about Kayla, about your mom, and me not telling you about *it*, but it has to be noisy."

"Like how?"

"Like in traffic, so it gets eaten up by the horns or the squeaks the train brakes make. You can't talk about it here, by the water. It's too nice here. I just want to say I think you're awesome. Don't say anything. I always have to get the last word." She put her head on my shoulder and turned her face up to the sun and closed her eyes and pet Flip blind.

When I got home, nobody was at the dinner table. Tonight was delivery food from the Palace of Enchantment, except it was all laid out real neat on platters. Mom and I usually ate right from the cartons. Leo was eating in front of the TV, some ESPN show. Aunt Jeanie was in the other room, at Mom's desk, eating in front of her iPad. "Sorry I'm late," I said.

"C'mon, champ," Leo said, "you don't have to worry about that with me." I fed Flip and then myself, and then we loaded the car with boxes and bags. I turned back for a last look at the apartment building, my bedroom window, the fire escape where the pigeons used to bunch up in the early morning. The old man upstairs threw out crumbs at sunrise. I closed my eyes and pretended really hard that I heard the cooing, that I heard Mom's voice. *You and I will never disappear. We are forever.* I opened my eyes and she wasn't there of course.

Aunt Jeanie fussed with my hair. She wasn't a musser. More of a fixer. "You forget something up there, Ben?"

"Nothing."

"Don't cry," she said, crying.

"Don't worry," I said. "I won't." And I didn't. We got into the car and left.

20
THE HOUSE BY THE CEMETERY

"You think you'll be all right in here, champ?"

It used to be Aunt Jeanie's workout room. We moved her treadmill and exercise balls down to the cellar. "I don't want to push you out of here," I said. "I'd feel better in the basement."

"Absolutely not," Aunt Jeanie said. "Your asthma. There's no air down there. I mean, of course it's fine for when I run for a few minutes."

"I don't know why you don't run outside, babe," Leo said.

"This is a total pain for you," I said. "Flip and me barging in on you like this."

"Nah, c'mon, now," Leo said.

"I just want to say thanks. Seriously. I'll pay for Flip's food, mine too."

"Champ, relax."

"I make around fifty bucks a week from my coupon deliveries."

"Now, now," Aunt Jeanie said. She looked like she wanted

to say more but didn't know what to say. She chewed her lip. She patted my back, leaning away. "Well, if you need us, we're right down the hall."

Leo yawned and stretched on his way out. "So happy to be home," he said.

The room was a lot smaller than my old one. The window looked over the cemetery. It sounds crummy, but it was okay, lots of pine trees. I couldn't see them so great in the night, but their shadows were sparkly in the moonlight. Mom got cremated, so now I wouldn't be able to visit her. They take the body after the funeral, and you don't see it again. Then later they send you her ashes, except how can you be sure they're hers? They were supposed to come back any day now.

Aunt Jeanie had made the bed so it was tucked really tight. I remembered the day we had the big talk, Mom, Jeanie and me. I can't remember why Leo wasn't there. The talk where Mom asked Jeanie if she would take care of me if she died. Jeanie clutched her heart—always clutching her heart—and her eyes got wet. "I'm so touched, really," she said. "That you think I would be a good, you know, that I could take care of Ben. Leo and I, kids, we just never had the time. Well, you know." "I know, sweetheart," Mom said to her. "But you make the time, and they give you more time than they take. Good time, they give you. You have a huge heart, Jeanie. Bigger than you know." "It's such an honor to be asked," Jeanie said. "So I'm gonna put you down for a yes then," Mom said. "Not that I'm planning on going any time soon. Just in case. Right, Ben?" She mussed my hair, and then Jeanie fixed it, but they both winked at me, and the same way too, like only sisters can. It was nice, except, just like Mom said, none of us really imagined it would happen. Not before I grew up anyway. Before I went out on my own.

I stared at the empty wall of my new room and wondered where I ought to hang my Chewbacca poster. Flip looked from me to the wall, trying to figure out what I was staring at. I set the big picture of Laura on the desk. I had a small one of me and Mom with the beach in the background on a sunny day. I pushed the pictures together. Laura was like twenty times bigger than me and Mom. I looked away and started to get mad at myself for getting teary. *Never let the hill slow you down, Traveler*, Mom used to say, except she wouldn't have minded me being sad. Then again, she would have cheered me up. I just didn't want to get started on that whole thing. You know, feeling sorry for myself. Once you start up on that, it's harder and harder to stop, and then before you know it you're a zombie.

I went to the kitchen to get Flip a bowl of water. Leo was eating over the sink. "There's crumb cake but no milk," he said with his mouth full.

"Thanks, I'm okay," I said.

Flip sat behind me and stared through my legs at Leo.

"He's pretty goofy-looking," Leo said. "He know any tricks?"

"Flip, box," I said, and Flip got into a match with his invisible opponent.

"That's hilarious." Leo got down on the floor and feinted jabs with Flip. And then he connected with a soft but quick slap across Flip's muzzle.

Flip ran behind me and kept sneezing. Leo crawled like a lizard toward Flip and Flip whimpered.

"I don't think he likes that too much," I said.

"We were just playing." He mussed Flip's head and stood up a little out of breath. "It's weird, you not calling me anything, you know? Dad would be weirder though, right? Unc? No? How's about just call me Leo then, okay? You want to watch TV or something?"

"School tomorrow."

"Hey, I can take of care of him for you. Trip, I mean. While you're at school."

"Thanks, but you don't have to." What, like I'm going to leave Flip with him after he just slapped him? Was he out of his mind? "I walk him for a long time in the morning and then when I get home. Um, I don't mean to say anything, but his name's, like, Flip."

"I never had a dog before," Leo said. "C'mere, pup." Flip didn't.

"He'll just sleep on the bed till I get back here," I said. "You don't have to worry about him at all. Really, Leo. I appreciate it though."

"I guess you have it all figured out then." He shrugged. "Sleep good." He went into his office, which was packed with boxes. He sold golf stuff on eBay, mostly those loser hats with the flap that covers your neck, shirts with humorous sayings, except I didn't get why they were funny. Like the one he was wearing that night was:

PH

GO~~LF~~ER

His specialty was gently used clubs, he said.

Flip and I settled down on top of the covers. No way was I going to be able to make that bed as perfectly as Aunt Jeanie did. I texted Halley the address of the therapy dog certification place. Leo was watching TV on the other side of the wall, and he laughed really loud. Flip shivered and hid in my armpit.

I called Chucky. "Is your mom there?"

"This isn't some wink thing, is it?"

"Chucky, be realistic for like a third of a second."

"You saying my mom's ugly?"

"Of course not. Your mom's really pretty."

"Watch it, Coffin."

While I was talking to him, my phone blipped with a text back from Halley: ♥

I didn't sleep. I watched my phone alarm tick down toward 4:30. Somebody was opening and closing cabinets in the kitchen. After that stopped I got up and made Flip breakfast.

Aunt Jeanie had left one of those padded cooler bags in the fridge. The note said,

Ben,

Not sure if Tess used to make you lunch.

If you'd rather get lunch at school, I won't be offended.

Sincerely,

Aunt Jeanie

It was a turkey and tomato sandwich on like seventy-grain bread or whatever and loaded down with avocado and sprouts and these things that looked like mutant mouse turds but were actually seeds, I hope. The whole thing was wrapped in waxed paper as tight as the sheets on the bed. I was starving and ate it right then. It was good even though it was healthy. I grabbed the pet carrier backpack, and Flip and I hustled to the subway.

There were no seats on the train. Half the people wore fast-food uniforms and slept standing up. The train ran slow because people kept holding the doors. I missed my transfer. When it came, that train was packed. I practically had to shove people to get out when my stop came. I knew I was going to need it, so I took a hit off my inhaler, and then I ran with Flip lockstep next to me to pick up my coupons, and then we *really* ran to get them delivered in time. Flip's tail wouldn't stop wagging, like all of this rushing around was terrific fun.

By the time I finished the coupons I was totally sweaty, and by the time I got to Chucky's I was ready for a nap, and it wasn't even seven in the morning.

21
DOGGY DAYCARE

"Mrs. Mold, I want to pay you for this," I said.

"Don't be ridiculous, Coffin," she said. "Molly and Ginger will love the company—especially GinGin. Now, you and Charles get your fannies to school." She took Flip into her arms.

"I'm coming back, Flip," I said. "I promise."

He licked my face and whimpered and then Mrs. Mold closed the door. I wasn't in that house for even a minute and already I was a little wheezy.

I fell asleep in second period and then again in seventh. My face slipped through my hands and smacked the desk. Rayburn wasn't in school that day either, though. I was pretty sure he wasn't coming back. I was used to it, seeing people disappear. Except you never got used to it. And then you had the ones who were always in your face.

I was at the water fountain when Angelina came up behind me and knocked me into the stream a little, so the water went down my sweatshirt. She'd stuck gum in the hole too, to make the water shoot into your eye. Why do people think that stuff is funny? Ronda wasn't laughing, though. She rolled her eyes. Come to think of it, Ronda never laughed. Never smiled either.

After school I ditched Chucky with the chess club geeks and hurried toward the Mold house. I stopped to pick up some donuts for the girls. One of them opened the door with Flip in her arms. She said, "Ooh, chocolate," grabbed the donuts, gave me Flip and shut the door. I headed off. The door swung open and Mrs. Mold called me back. "Coffin, check this out." She showed me a bunch of videos on her phone. Here was Flip's day:

First, he got an ear treatment from Ginger.

Then he wrestled around with the three-year-old girl. "That's Charlene," Mrs. Mold said. "No, wait, Charlotte."

Then Flip cuddled into the golden retriever's armpit for a nap.

Next, Flip found the garbage bin, and he spent a good five minutes investigating a diaper. Mrs. Mold giggled the whole time she videoed him.

Later the dogs went out into the small weedy patch of cement that was the Mold yard and played chase, sort of. Flip ran up to old Molly and nipped her neck and took off. The retriever wagged her tail and limped a few steps after Flip, who tore around the yard in circles.

The next video was Flip at the window in a staring contest with a pigeon.

Then at noon one of the girls came home from kindergarten and dressed Flip in a doll nightgown and put a bunch of ribbons in his hair, and he didn't mind at all.

In the last video, Flip, Molly, and Ginger the cat are sprawled out on the couch. They're snoring, and Flip is on his back with all four legs out like an upside-down flying squirrel. He wakes up and yawns and shakes himself off and goes to the front door and sits. He cocks his head. Then three minutes later his crooked little tail starts wagging, and a minute after that I show up with the donuts.

"Flip!" Halley said. Pink beret today. The button was a strawberry. She scooped him up and we went into the therapy dog certification place.

My teacher gave Flip a chew stick, and then she said, "Not yours." Flip cocked his head, but he didn't drop the stick. The teacher told me to try. The way I learned it from the library book was to say, "Leave it." Flip dropped the stick. The teacher put down a cookie. Flip went for it. "Leave it," I said, and he turned away from it and trotted to me and sat and gave me his paw.

Halley hooted and clapped and said, "Woohoo Flip!"

Next was to make sure Flip didn't freak when he heard a loud noise, like if a kid shrieked. My teacher had me read to Flip. Behind his back she dropped an aluminum pan. Flip spun toward the clatter.

"Flip, I got it," I said. He turned right back to me and sat and listened to me read. Next time the pan clattered, Flip's ears went up, but he didn't spin around. "I got it," I said, and he lay down.

Next was the most fun. My teacher's daughter, seven years old, sat on the floor and read to Flip. He cocked his head every time the girl said, "Right Flip?"

I got him to do this little trick I taught him. I said, "Flip, who wants a belly scratch?"

Flip tucked himself into the girl's lap and rolled over into the upside-down flying squirrel pose. His tail swept the floor probably a hundred times a minute.

"This guy has the gift," my teacher said.

"He's a traveler," I said.

"She was talking about *you*, moron," Halley said.

Flip licked the girl's cheeks, then her lips.

"I can get him to stop that," I told my teacher, but truth told, I was having a hard time getting him to not make out with every person he ever met.

22

THE MAGICIAN
WHO RIDES THE MOON

Halley and I got tacos and went to the plaza near the dog training place and watched this skateboarder girl in baggy army clothes do crazy awesome tricks. Halley fed Flip chicken bits. "I swear he's trying to tell me something," she said. "Look, you can see yourself in his eyes. Flip, what is it, boy?"

"You should call her Halley," I said. "The novella, the girl on the trapeze? Your name's the most awesome ever."

"It really is, isn't it? Still, it'll be too confusing. We'll call her Helen, as in Helen of Troy. You know, from the *Iliad*?"

"I skimmed the SparkNotes."

"She was the woman who was so beautiful that all the Greeks and Trojans went psycho killing each other over her. Perfect, yes? I'm not really asking you. Just nod. Good. Now, the electrician dude. Gimme a hero's name than begins with *B*."

"Bruce," I said. "As in Wayne? Hello, Batman?"

"I'm looking for classical Greco-Roman tragedy, and you give me comic books. You want to be Bruce, fine. Either way, he's you."

"Wow."

"What now?"

"I'm flattered I made it into your story."

"*Our* story," she said. "I've decided we're writing this together."

"No way. I suck at stories."

"You read like a vampire who feeds on ink. I need your help on this. Even if I write a book a year, I have a lot of catching up to do if I'm going to pump out a hundred and eleven before I die. You and me, twice as fast, twice as fun. And if you suck I'll fire you, if that will make you feel better. Look, Flip's doing the UDFSP for me." That's what she called the upside-down flying squirrel pose. "What, Flip? What are you trying to tell me, you freaky little banana?"

"The Helen and Bruce in the book," I said. "Just friends, right?"

"*Best* friends. Okay, so here's what I have so far. It's night. Luna Park is closed. Bruce the electrician kid is hanging out on the platform with all the lights that light up the trapeze ride. The magician's with him."

"We're totally calling him Mercurious, right?" I said.

"You have to ask? Mercurious and Bruce are watching the trapeze girl."

"Helen."

"Yup. She's at the top of the pole, getting ready to swing. Bruce has her lit up with a spotlight that's as bright as the moon. He's worried. So's Mercurious. It looks like the gorgeous Helen is unclipping her safety cables."

"Why?" I said.

"That's what Bruce the superhero electrician wants to know too. Helen calls out from her platform, 'The problem with the safety wires is you can only swing so far before the wires rein you in. I need to see how high I can go. I'll never be great if I don't know what it's like to soar free.' She swings away from the platform, and up, up until she's as high as the stars. The world is so beautiful from up there, Ben. Everything is sparkly, the moon on the waves, the city itself, lit silver and gold. Suddenly Helen realizes she's flown higher than she ever could have imagined, and she gets scared. Her hands sweat and slip away from the bar."

"Bruce runs as fast as he can off the end of the spotlight platform," I said. "He catches Helen."

"My hero! Except, duh, now they're *both* falling—until time stops."

"Hold on a second," I said. "Time can't stop. It's mathematically impossible."

"Math shmath; in our story, time can stop, and it does," Halley said. "Bruce and Helen stop falling. The ocean freezes. It's like a snapshot. Luna Park fades to gold."

"Luna Park 1905?"

"Exactly. They're not *out* of time at all. They've slipped through one of the little cracks in it, the ones between each moment. The golden tower rises up to meet them. They're in the top of it now, and the sky warms up with silky blond light. The stars spin out of place, into the pattern of the shooting stars on Mercurious's cape. He's sitting on the moon. 'Well now,' he says to Helen and Bruce, 'look at the mess you've gotten yourselves into.'"

"And?" I said. "What happens next?"

"Only the greatest adventure ever." Halley shrugged. "We'll figure it out as we go."

"This is cool, you bouncing ideas off me like this," I said.

"I totally have to talk it all into my phone before we forget." And she did. When she was done, she put a chicken nugget on her lips and leaned down so she was eye to eye with Flip. Of course he ate the chicken right off her lips.

"Feeding him from your mouth like that isn't helping me to get him to stop kissing people."

"Why would you ever want him to stop?" she said.

The skateboarder girl did a backflip and the crowd cheered. The rush hour trains rumbled under the street. The bus brakes sounded like elephant calls. "So, it's definitely noisy here," I said.

She nodded. "I still don't want to talk about it."

"Okay. I just want to make sure you're, like, okay."

"Ben, I'm kicking this thing's butt. Seriously, I am. I feel it. I'm going to get myself to the point I have zero cancer in my body. Then all I have to do is stay clear for five years, and they're going to tell me they're almost positive it's never coming back. Now hold my freezing cold hand, no more talking."

We held hands and watched this boat-like cloud fly past the sun.

"Are you thinking what I'm thinking?" she said.

"You want to put a cloud ship into the story," I said.

"Mind reader."

"How about a spaceship?"

"I *knew* you were going to turn this into a sci-fi," she said. "Okay, spaceship, but then I get to put in another magician."

"We'll call her the Contessa of Starlight," I said. "Tess for short."

"Yes, and her wand is made of roentgenium."

"Except maybe it's more like a magic staff," I said. "Yeah, she has the littlest limp, a pinch of arthritis maybe, but you'll never catch her complaining about it—or anything else either. That's why everybody loves her. She takes the tough stuff that comes her way, and instead of letting it push her down, she picks herself up. She picks up everybody around her and carries them up the mountain."

"She's sounds amazing, Ben Coffin. She sounds awesome. She's my kind of hero, the perfect character for our story. I knew there was a reason I hired you."

23

LEO MEANS LION

"Hi," I said.

Aunt Jeanie was on the phone. Leo was on the couch. He didn't say hi. He pouted and went into his office. Aunt Jeanie hung up the phone.

"Did I do something wrong?" I said.

"He was . . . *sad* that you didn't trust him with the dog."

"It's not that," I said.

Leo leaned out of his office. "It's *exactly* that," he said. "I may look stupider than I am, champ, but I'm not, okay? When did they start letting people bring dogs into school anyway?"

I told them about the Mold situation. "It's just easier for everybody," I said. "I exercise him while I deliver my coupons, and then there's another dog and all these kids for him to play with."

"*Easier,*" Leo said. "Right, *that's* the reason, Jeanie. It's *easier.*" He huffed back into his office and closed the door.

Aunt Jeanie patted the barstool next to hers and I sat. She took out one of those lint roller things and rolled it over my shirt to get the dog hair off. "I want to tell you a secret," she said. "You have to keep this just between you and me. The word *Leo* means lion. He has a lion's heart. Big. Sensitive, you know? He wounds easily. Ben, I want you to be as comfortable as you can be here. We all need to work on our trust, right?"

"I do trust you."

"I'm not so sure you do. It's horrifying, losing Tess so suddenly. Life is just awful sometimes, even most times. We have to be realistic about that and avoid the rough patches as best we can, you know? Even if you don't need Leo, pretend you do a little, okay?"

"Actually, I do need him," I said.

I knocked on Leo's office door. It opened fast. He nodded at me, like what did I want now?

"I need a sponsor for my therapy dog certification test," I said.

He frowned, then he shrugged. "Okay." He put out his huge hand. I shook it. "You want to play a video game?" he said. It was this racecar thing on his computer, totally from a million years ago. He was the type who *really* liked to win. Flip hunkered under my arm, on the opposite side of Leo. His shirt said: KEEP CALM, CADDY ON. *Wha?* He caught me looking at it. "Hilarious, right?" he said. "Here, I'll get you one."

"That's okay."

"It's no problem, really. I have boxes full of them."

"Cool," I said.

"Champ, speaking of boxes, maybe you want to go through those books and figure out which ones you want to sell. I don't mind, but Jeanie's a little nutty about stuff lying around the basement. She's kind of a control freak. *Neat* freak, I mean. Don't tell her I called her a control freak, whatever you do."

"Never."

"Us bonding like this, two guys keeping secrets? It's fun, right?"

24
THE TEST

Flip and I trained all that night and then the next day after school at the park. Halley had to do some last-minute paperwork stuff with her mom to get the final okay from the Read to Rufus people that we could set up the program at the library, but she was definitely going to be with Flip and me for the test the next day, which was Rosh Hashanah, so no school. The test was at ten thirty, the last appointment available until November. I couldn't wait that long. The Read to Rufus people said the kids were psyched and ready to go, as soon as Flip passed the test.

I woke early that morning of Rosh Hashanah, of the test. I probably didn't sleep the night before either. I wore the shirt Leo gave me to make him happy. I brushed Flip so he'd look sharp for the test. Aunt Jeanie got her lint roller out and picked up the like two hairs that fell on the carpet before she went to work. I took Flip for a good long walk and fed him some cheddar bits. It was nine forty-five, and there was no sign of Leo.

I went to the bedroom door and knocked, and then I knocked louder. Nothing. I went in. Flip hung back in the hallway. "Thanks pal," I said.

Leo looked dead, except dead people don't snore so loud you feel like Darth Maul's jabbing your eardrums with a serraknife. I shook his foot, hard. "Leo? Leo!"

I sat on the edge of the bed. I guess I wasn't surprised. Expecting to be let down didn't make it hurt any less. Just when you think things are maybe going to be okay, why does everything have to get messed up?

I called Halley to tell her the bad news. She was pretty mad. She wanted me to take a pair of cymbals and smash them together right by Leo's ear, except who ever has any cymbals lying around? *"Okay, look, we're not going to be defeated,"* she said. *"Just get on the train and get over there. I have an idea."*

Halley was waiting for us out front. So was Mercurious. He must have come from teaching a magic class, because he was still in his sparkly purple sweat suit. He wore a glittery Brooklyn Cyclones baseball cap. Halley wore no cap. Instead she wore a bright pink wig, a short one, with the hair spiked up. She looked totally freaking awesome. "Um, that shirt," she said.

"I know," I said.

"'Caddy on'?"

"I have no idea either."

"Never mind. Let's do this."

We went in. "Huddle up," Halley said. The three humans held hands, and Flip stuck his paw in there too. "Coffin? You rock. Flip? You rule. Take no prisoners. I have no idea what that means. Whatever. Dad, any words for the boys?"

He mussed my hair. "Just remember this one thing," he said. "Okay?"

"You're magic."

The testing guy called out, "Ben Coffin?" His name tag said Mr. Thompkins. I said, "Thanks Mr. Thompkins," and stuck out my hand to shake his.

"For what?" he said, and he didn't shake my hand. "The examination shall commence in five seconds, four, three, two, one."

We had to pass nine things. Here's what they were.

1. GREET THE TESTER. Flip gave the guy his paw. Check.

2. STAY. I told him to, and then I walked away. He looked sort of totally suicidal and slumped to the floor, but he stayed. Bingo.

3. COME. Like he wouldn't?

4. IGNORE THE STRANGER. Some really mad-looking guy came in yelling about how somebody stole his bicycle. Flip checked him out until I said, "Flip, I got it." Flip kept his eyes on me. Halley mouthed "Nice!" and Mr.

Lorentz clapped until Thompkins said, "No encourage-
ment allowed. *Thank* you." He did a double take on Mr.
Lorentz's sparkly purple clothes.

5. VISIT A SICK PERSON. Thompkins sat in a wheelchair.
   "Go say hi, Flip." He went to the chair and leaned into the
   tester's leg.

6. STARTLE. Thompkins tried the old drop-the-aluminum
   pan trick. Flip yawned.

7. LEAVE IT. Puh-lease.

8. MEETING ANOTHER DOG. A German shepherd came
   into the room. Flip trotted up to her, sniffed her butt and
   then rolled over at her feet into the upside-down flying
   squirrel pose.

9. APPROPRIATE AFFECTION. Here it was, the one place
   we could fail. Thompkins sat on the floor and called Flip
   over. Flip sat at Thompkins's feet. "Flip, cuddle," I said. He
   nestled into the grump's lap. Just when I thought we were
   home free, Flip reached up to Thompkins's face and stuck
   his tongue in the old man's mouth. Thompkins made a
   yuck face. Halley and Mr. Lorentz looked like they were
   watching a ship sink.

Thompkins went to his desk and frowned while he wrote
all over his stupid test sheet. He stamped it really hard and
called me over. "I suppose the gentleman in the lavender
exercise apparel is your sponsor?" he said.

"Yup."

He waved over Mercurious. "Sign here, please." Then he passed the paper to me and told me to sign it. This is what it looked like.

THIS LICENSE CONFERS TO HANDLER THE LEGAL RIGHT TO BRING THE THERAPY ANIMAL NAMED HERE INTO HOSPITALS, SCHOOLS AND ANY SUCH ESTABLISHMENTS WHERE THE ANIMAL'S GIFTS ARE NEEDED OR DESIRED.

HANDLER: BEN COFFIN

SPONSOR: MICHAEL LORENTZ

THERAPY ANIMAL: FLIP COFFIN

There was another page, a SPECIAL COMMENDATION. Thompkins wrote, *Mr. Coffin exhibits true grace with Flip. Rarely have I seen such genuine trust between man and dog. I expect this exceptional dog and his equally exceptional handler will go on to mend many hearts. The world is about to become a lovelier place.*

Halley put up her fist for a pound. I bumped her knuckles. "You *so* slay," she said. When I bumped Mercurious's knuckles, sparks shot up from his fist, but not like the Santa magician's sparks, the ones that came out of the magic box. Those were blood-colored, and Halley's dad's were pink and blue and softer, quieter, like a whisper instead of a scream.

Halley scooped up Flip and we went outside and then the craziest thing happened.

A pigeon's shadow raced up the side of a building and met the pigeon on the ledge, and *that's* when I cried, and so hard I thought my eyes might drip out of my head. I know, it was just some totally random thing that set me off, but it was really beautiful. Like even when the bird was darting about here and there so fast, all up in the air, her shadow was always with her, even though she couldn't see it. But when she landed, there it was, touching her again. This would have been the best day of my life if my mom was here to see it. I didn't say that to Halley and Mercurious, though, and I didn't need to. They hugged me and patted my back and didn't say "It's okay," and I really appreciated that.

25
THE LAUNCHPAD

The Lorentzes invited me and Flip over for Rosh Hashanah. "You'll eat so much you'll totally be puking all over yourself," Halley said.

"Sounds great," I said. I called Aunt Jeanie and she said no problem, because she was working late anyway. I didn't tell her Leo overslept, and I guess he didn't either, because she didn't say anything about it. I thought she forgot about the test, until right after I said bye, she said, *"Wait, how'd the dog do?"*

"He passed."

"Oh, that's wonderful, Ben. I was worried."

"Why?"

"Well, I just was. You know." I really didn't know. *"I'm sure Tess is proud of you, watching us from above. Right?"*

"Uh-huh."

"Very proud. Yes, you go and enjoy yourself now. Be polite and thankful."

"I will."

"Good. Good. Okay, good-bye."

The Lorentzes' apartment was nice, tons of books. The paintings were Halley's from when she was in pre-K until now. My favorite was this one of the planet Mercury. Her dad was standing on it. His arms pointed to the sky, and he waved a baton like he was conducting the stars.

Halley's room was wall-to-wall novels. She had every freaking edition of *Jane Eyre* ever printed, like one wasn't more than enough. Flip jumped onto her bed, and she jumped onto it after him while I checked out her books. "I read *Iron Man*, like you told me to," she said. "How is it that I, a sophisticated young woman with near paranormal intelligence, am totally crushing on a cheesy comic book character? You're having a spectacularly negative effect on my reading life."

"You're welcome," I said. "Let's keep working on the novella. What's the title, by the way?"

"I've been thinking really hard about this. Don't freak out. I want to call it *The Magic Box*."

"Hm," I said.

"Ben, we're going to take the most negative thing in your life and turn it into the treasure you meant it to be."

"How?"

"Okay, it's like this: Bruce and Helen have slipped through

a crack in time, and now they're back in the old Luna Park, right? The one from 1905."

"*Dreamland at Night.*"

"Yupper. Mercurious tells Bruce and Helen there's only one way to survive their fall. They have to get to the exact moment before Helen decided to swing without the safety wires, and instead, she and Bruce will go to McDonald's and stuff themselves with Oreo cookie McFlurries and talk about their favorite books."

"Like, they get a do-over?" I said.

"Exactly."

"So how do they get from 1905 back to the minute before Helen jumped from the platform?"

"It turns out that the golden tower of light from 1905 is actually a spaceship."

"Love it," I said.

"Knew you would!"

"The spaceship is going to take Bruce and Helen to the Contessa of Starlight."

"Go on?"

"Yeah, see, she's the only one who knows how to get Helen and Bruce back to the right place in time, to where they can skip the whole trapeze thing and go for McFlurries instead. Problem is, she's really far away, the Contessa, on a different planet, doing the speech therapy thing."

"Of course. Which planet?" Halley said.

"It's not even in our solar system," I said. "It's hidden in a whole other star cluster. The secret to its location is in the library, of course. They'll need to head to the Branch for Interstellar Travel, which is the main attraction on Libris, a newly discovered moon of Neptune."

"I love Neptune. It's the most awesome shade of blue."

"Which is totally why I picked it," I said. "There they'll seek the guidance of—"

"Penny, Keeper of the Star Maps."

"Your mom's name is Penny? The women in your family have seriously good names."

"I know."

"Penny the librarian. Cool."

"Technically they're called media specialists."

"Technically I need applesauce if we don't want the latkes to taste like I burned them a little," Interstellar Media Specialist Penny Lorentz called to us from the kitchen. We went out and got the sauce and hurried back for the feast.

26
HALLEY'S RAP

The latkes were the size of waffles. We all snuck Flip pieces of brisket, which made no sense since everybody knew everybody else was sneaking. After dessert we played Scrabble for Cheez-Its and blue M&M'S. Mr. Lorentz started whistling a song from the musical *Man of La Mancha*, Halley told me. It was Mercurious's favorite apparently, and then Mrs. Lorentz started singing the words, and before you knew it we all were singing about this old man who never gives up, who keeps on keeping on no matter how bad things get, and then Halley said, "I feel a song coming on, a Halley Lorentz original if you please, oh yes I do."

"Then sing it," Mercurious said.

"Poppers, bass beat please," she said. He laid it down, like really getting into it with some serious head bopping, and then she said, "Okay that's actually totally adorably lame, but it will suffice." Then she rapped:

Got me a bestie, his name's Ben.

He can't see it, but he kills with the pen.

Poet don't know it, you've heard that before,

My boy's got stories, paste you to the floor.

He saved a dog, see, a friend to the end.

He saves me daily, Halley Lorentz.

How you heal me, you and mighty mutt Flip?

All's I can say is you make me feel hip.

Bad comes to worse, and you don't give in.

You don't mope or lose hope, you honor your kin.

You hustle those coupons come rain or shine.

You keep on keeping on in the toughest of times.

Rosh Hashanah means New Year, new wonder—
you'll see.

Mom and Mercurious, Flip, you and me.

She raised her glass of sparkling cider. "Shanah Tovah, everybody. Happy New Year. I'm so grateful that we're all here together."

Her mom patted my back and said quietly, "Yes, we're *all* here. We're *here*." She touched her fingertip to my heart. Then she messed up my hair the way Mom used to and kissed my forehead and hugged me and didn't let go.

Mercurious pointed to the window. A gold laser beam pulsed from his finger and hit the glass, and a silent explosion of fireworks lit up the sky over Brighton Beach and in the distance Luna Park. *Dreamland at Night.* I knew it was only video projection, but it was shiny and beautiful and I wanted it to be real. The rides were spinning and the lights whirled.

27

THE RINGSIDE SEAT

They drove me home in Mr. Lorentz's sparkly purple SUV, and the whole way there we sang *Man of La Mancha*, and then that turned into pop songs, then somehow Christmas carols—in September—and then Halley's song. Flip tried to sing along too. "He's halfway between howling and that warbling sound Gizmo makes in *Gremlins*," Halley said. The more we laughed at him, the more he did it.

The Mercurious-mobile pulled up to the house, and I pretended I wasn't the third saddest I'd ever been, having to get out of that car. The house lights were off, and the Lorentz family waited for me to get inside before they drove away. I clicked on the light and Flip whimpered. Leo was sitting on the couch—just sitting there, no TV, no iPad or music. I said hi and he shook his head. His eyes were glassy. "Jeanie's pretty mad."

"Why? What'd I do?" I said.

"At *me*. Why didn't you wake me up?"

"I tried, I swear."

"Then you didn't try hard enough," he said. He was talking funny, quiet, slow-motion. "I thought I hit snooze, but I hit off instead."

"It worked out anyway."

"For *you* it worked out," he said. "I look like the bad guy now. To her anyhow. Speak of the devil."

Aunt Jeanie came in with red wet eyes. "Hi," she said. She had a pretty wooden box under her arm, a little bigger than the one that triggered Kayla's asthma attack.

"What's in the box?" Leo said.

She did a double take on him. "How could you, Leo?" she said. "I can smell it from here. I'm *not* going through this again."

"For cripe's sake Jeanie, relax, it was one freaking beer."

"It *wasn't* one."

"You have to embarrass me in front of the kid?"

"You embarrass yourself."

"A guy can't even have a couple of drinks in his own house once every five years?" He got up and went to his office and shut the door and turned up the TV loud enough so we could hear it through the wall. Two wrestlers yelled about how they were going to mangle each other once they got into the ring. Aunt Jeanie sat on the couch and tried not to cry. "I'm sorry you had to see that."

"It's okay," I said.

"It's not," she said. "It's not."

I sat next to her. Flip shivered at my feet. I wanted to pick him up, but Aunt Jeanie had a rule of no dogs on the couch. She put the box on the coffee table. "Tess," she said.

"Oh," I said. "That's like . . ."

"Like what?"

"I don't know."

"I don't either," she said. "I really don't." She breathed in slowly and then breathed out fast and choppy and cried. I put my hand on her shoulder. "Thank you," she said. She held my hand for a second, squeezed it, and then put it on my lap and patted it and took her hand away. "It's late," she said. "You don't want to fall asleep in school tomorrow."

We were off for Rosh Hashanah again but I said, "Definitely not. Good night." I couldn't get away from those ashes fast enough. I forced myself not to run to my room. Flip stuck so close to my feet I was tripping over him.

"Ben?" she said. "I'm glad it went well today. With the dog, I mean."

"Thank you." I closed the door and then my eyes and I counted. I figured maybe I'd get to ten before it started, but it kicked in at six. I couldn't hear exactly what Leo and Aunt Jeanie were screaming at each other, but it was louder than the wrestlers.

Less than four years. That's how long we had to last before I'd be allowed to go live on my own, legally. I was a year ahead in school, and if I kept working really hard I could make up another one and graduate at sixteen. Flip and I would get the heck out of the city and tag along with Halley to the same college, and she and I would take the same English classes and become writing partners—except they probably didn't let you bring dogs into the dorm rooms.

28
ROCKS AND BOOKS

The next day was like the night before never happened. Leo and I went to Home Depot and bought bags of rocks and spread them out in the tiny yard. "It's a rock garden," he said. "I guess you figured that out. You're a good worker, running those coupon deliveries at the crack of dawn, helping me now."

"You too."

"I been at it a long time," he said. "I'll die working. You though, always studying the way you do, I think you just might make it."

"Make what?"

"Champ, you like golf?"

"Mini."

"That's not a crime. Yet. *Ha.* I can teach you how to play real golf, you know? Maybe we'll go to the driving range sometime." He farted and covered his mouth for some reason. "'Scuse me. I'll be back." He went in.

Jeanie came out with lemonade. "He's sick from the beer. Serves him right." She was looking at me like she wanted me to say something. I shrugged. She sat and patted the porch step for me to sit next to her. "I ordered an angel figurine online. It looks like marble but it's actually highly durable polyurethane. They make bowling balls out of this stuff. It'll be here tomorrow."

"That's, like, great," I said.

"Yes. Well, I'd like to bury her under it. Tess. Back here. I should have asked you first."

"Asked me what?"

"If you were okay with that. You know, burying her ashes."

"I never really thought about it," I said. "I guess we have to put them somewhere. Are you allowed, though? Like isn't there a law or something, that maybe she's supposed to go into a, you know, cemetery?"

"I don't think so. I just feel like she'll be closer to us this way."

"Right."

"You don't think so?"

"No, no, I do. It's nice, your plan."

"Good then?"

"Good, yeah."

"Great." She patted my back, and I could tell she was working hard not to lean away. "I can help you sort through those book boxes, if you want."

"I'll finish up today."

"Oh Ben, the dog looks like he's going to pee in the rocks. No, dog. Shoo. *Shoo.*"

Halley came over to help me go through my books. Jeanie was at work and more importantly Leo was in Manhattan to see his foot doctor. Chucky kept texting me to send him a picture of Halley. "I keep seeing the word *butt* in that text stream," she said.

"You never told me why we're going to call the story *The Magic Box*," I said.

"It's like this: Tess is gonna help Bruce and Helen, but *she* needs their help too. The planet she's on? It's called Mundum Nostrum, and it's total war there. Tess is trying to get the Nostrumians to settle their differences by, hello, learning how to talk to each other again. See what I did there, working in the speech therapy?" She patted herself on the back. "This requires some serious magic, the kind Tess keeps in her totally gorgeous penthouse apartment back on Earth, in the top of the golden tower from Luna Park 1905, in this beautiful wooden box."

"So what's in the box?"

"Only the greatest treasure that has ever existed."

"An antigravity belt that lets you fly? A wearable technology that lets you be invisible?"

"You're such a *boy*. It's *so* much more awesome than

those." She dropped a pile of books on top of the To Go pile.

"Seriously, you're making me get rid of my *X-Men: First Class*?"

"Let somebody else enjoy it," she said. "Hey? You nervous?"

"About what?"

"Monday." She lit up that dingy basement with the biggest lopsided smile. Monday was our first Read to Rufus session with the little kids. "Flip, Flip, Flip, Flip, Flip!" She picked him up and spun around with him.

"Champ, that you down there?" Leo said. He limped into the basement.

"Hi, I'm Halley."

"Hi. Yeah, I thought that voice was a little high for Ben," Leo said. He stared a little too long at her pink wig.

"Well, I better get going," she said. "Gotta get home to help my dad with a show."

"What kind of *show*?" Leo said

"Magic act for a birthday party."

"Ah," Leo said.

"Very nice to meet you," she said. Her hand was tiny in his, but she gave a good shake.

Flip and I walked her to the train. When we got back, Leo said, "Tess didn't mind you hanging out with chicks like that?"

"Mom would have loved her," I said. "Besides, like what?"

"Forget about the pink dye job for now, in my day girls didn't cut their hair to look like boys. It's like she's trying to be in your face about it, you know what I mean?"

"No, I don't."

"She's purposely shocking people. She's drawing attention to herself. I'm doing it again, aren't I? Messing up. I'm only trying to look out for you here, champ. The people you let yourself be around? They're a reflection on *you*."

"Leo?"

"Yeah?"

Even his stupid shirt made me sick, not to mention totally confused me. It said: THREE! [I'M ALWAYS COMING UP A LIT-TLE SHORT.] All the synonyms for the word *idiot* lunged up from my stomach toward my throat, and they weren't about to get stuck in my heart this time. If I had anyplace else to live—anyplace at all—I would have called him every one of them too. "How's your foot?" I said.

29

READ TO RUFUS

Now I was glad to have my headphones back, even if Rayburn had worn them. I needed them to drown out Leo and Jeanie. They argued nonstop. That whole weekend they were going back and forth about Christmas vacation, Mexico again or Maine? I wondered if they were like this before Flip and I came into the picture. I didn't know what to do except stay in my room and study and tell myself that for every test I aced Flip and I were one step closer to getting out of Leo and Jeanie's. "Four years, Flip. Less than four. Three years, nine months and twenty days until I turn sixteen. We can hang in that long, right?"

He cocked his head and licked my lips. He was the best study partner. He really did love when you read to him. Monday morning I dropped him off at the Mold house. He looked a little sad as I left. "Come on now, Flip bud. You know I'll be back soon. I promise." As soon as he heard that, his tail started wagging again.

Monday after school Chucky and I hustled over to the Mold house to pick up Flip. "Ronda Glomski told me Rayburn isn't holding up his end of that contract they made him sign," Chucky said.

"He's not going to the guidance counselor?" I said.

"Nobody knows where he is. My mouth hurts every time I think about him."

"Then don't think about him." That's what Mom would've said.

"I seriously hope he dropped out. Dude, for real, how lame is this Read to Rufus thing going to be? Worse than chess club?"

"Halley's gonna be there."

"Okay, I'll come."

We trotted into the library and right upstairs to where they were waiting: the Read to Rufus lady, Mrs. Lorentz, three kids, a bunch of parents, a teacher, and Halley.

"Cheez Whiz crust," Chucky whispered to me. "Nice butt. Not bad in the chestal area either, Coffin. I mean, they could be bigger, but well done just the same."

"Any thoughts about her *face*?"

"Huh? Yeah, that too." Only then did he notice her wig, which she'd dyed in spiky stripes of color. "Okay, you were right: She's seriously as cool as a rainbow."

Flip jumped into her arms. "Ben, this is Brian," she said.

"I'm seven," the kid said, like he'd fight me if I said otherwise, except he didn't look me in the eye. He was small for seven, and the book he had was *The Dog Who Wanted to Become a Boy.* "I picked it because I figured he'd like it better than *The Velveteen Rabbit,* which maybe he'd want to eat." He nodded to Flip, who cocked his head. "It isn't mine though, the book. It's from the liberry. They made me carry it." He held it away from himself as far as he could, like it was a bag of dog turds.

"I'll hold it for you," I said, "if you hold Flip for me for a sec."

Halley put Flip into his arms, and Flip licked half a smile into the kid's lips. "His breath smells okay," he said. "It's not like rotten milk that much."

We sat on the couch. "Who told you *The Dog Who Wanted to Become a Boy* is one of Flip's all-time favorites?" I said.

"Serious?"

"You know what he also loves, Brian? When you say his name. After you read a little, just say, 'Right, Flip?' Read him your favorite part."

The kid looked me in the eye, but just for a second. "Thing is, it's at the end. It's not a happy ending, but it kind of is too."

"Those are the kind Flip likes the most. Read it if you don't believe me."

The kid read, and Flip was all eyes on him. "'I wanted to

be hum . . . hummm . . .'" He whispered, "What's this word again?"

"Human," I said.

"'I wanted to be human, because then the girl co . . . co-uh-luh-d . . .' Tell me."

"Could. That one's tricky. You're doing so awesome."

"'I wanted to be human, because then the girl could understand me. She was my best fri . . .'"

"You're doing great, Brian," I said. "Just sound it out letter by letter."

"'Fri-een-d—friend'?"

"You're totally amazing. Flip wants to give you a knuckle bump. Right, Flip?"

The kid put out his fist and Flip bumped him. His voice got louder. "'She was my best friend, and I had to tell her that.' Right, Flip?" Flip cocked his head almost ninety degrees. "I think he really is listening to me," the kid said. "'I was getting older and would not be around much longer,' Flip." Flip bumped him again and licked the kid's nose. They forgot I was there. The kid read and read, and Flip was fascinated. "'She told me so many times, in so many ways, that she loved me, and I tried to say it back with cuddles and kisses. I tried so hard. But it was not the same. I wanted to say the words, just once, to say I love you, so she would know.'"

Flip did a wiggle worm into the kid's lap and rolled over for a belly scratch.

Everybody clapped, and the kid got embarrassed and hid his face in Flip's neck. I looked out and Chucky nodded and Halley winked at me. Mercurious was there. He was holding Mrs. Lorentz's hand, and he gave me the thumbs-up. A rainbow-colored flame grew from the tip of his thumb.

Brian closed the book, and Flip put his head in the kid's lap. "The dog never becomes a boy," Brian said. "He never gets to say the words."

"But you said it was a happy ending too," I said.

"Yeah. It's happy because the girl knows anyway. You can just tell. She knows how he feels about her."

30

THE NEXT INSTALLMENT
OF *THE MAGIC BOX*

We got takeout slices with Chucky, and then Halley said Mold had to scram. "Why?" Chucky said.

"Because you need to go rest your eyes after staring at my, ahem, *chestal* area nonstop for the last two hours."

"It wasn't the *whole* two hours."

"Go. Ben and I have to work anyway."

"On what?"

"Our story of *The Magic Box*."

"Why's it magic?" Chucky said. "What's inside? C'mon, tell me."

Halley elbowed me. "That's one copy sold anyway." We went to our bench by Luna Park. "When last we saw our time-traveling alter egos, Bruce and Helen were trapped in a snapshot of 1905 with Mercurious, in the top of the golden tower," she said.

"Except the tower is actually a golden spaceship," I said.

"Maybe it rises off the ground and floats onto its side like a blimp."

"Okay, we're totally doing it. One little problem: Tess and the people of Mundum Nostrum need the magic box ASAP. How do we get a blimp to travel faster than the speed of light?"

"Easy. You use a quantum vector slingshot made of a dark matter neutrino alloy. Add a roentgenium booster, and you're moving a hundred and eleven thousand times the speed of light."

"You have my full attention now. Please proceed."

"Mercurious has buckets of the stuff, and he helps Helen and Bruce fuel up the golden blimp. 'As much as I want to go with you,' he says, 'I can't leave the people of Coney Island stranded—way too many bar mitzvahs this month. Tess is sending me mind waves that put the location of Mundum Nostrum somewhere in the constellation of Canis Major, in the orbit of Sirius.'"

"The Dog Star!" Halley said, scooping up Flip. "Helen and Bruce will need a seriously awesome pilot to get them there. Who better to guide them to Sirius than the mightiest therapy dog in existence? Flip, smooshy face." He gave her one and got his tongue all the way up into her mouth. "Mercurious gives Bruce the magic box. 'Okay, Travelers,' he says."

"'Travelers,'" I said. "Nice."

"'I know you really, really want to know what's inside,' Mercurious says, 'but promise me you won't open it.'"

"Why?" I said. "Shouldn't Helen and Bruce know their cargo?"

"Not in this case. This treasure is so spectacularly unique that Bruce and Helen can't possibly understand its true worth—not until Tess shows them how to wield it. Just to be sure they don't peek, Mercurious locks the box with a key made from sparks, the kind that shine in people's eyes after they witness a good deed. There's only one other copy of the key in existence."

"And Tess has it. Drats." It was really fun watching Halley get into it. She paced and talked everything into her phone and kind of hopped around. Truth told, that was more fun than the story part, which was kind of lame. I mean, transporting a magic box from one planet to another? It was like in every other comic I read. But seeing the Rainbow Girl get all smiley as we thought it up together? That was seriously fresh.

"Ben Coffin, are you ready for the journey to begin? I warn you, it's uphill all the way."

"Like I'd go with you on a downhill one? Flip, set a course for the moon Libris and the map room of Penny the sooth-saying media specialist."

"Speaking of which, my phone's buzzing and, yes, it's totally Mom texting me to get my butt home to go to yoga with her. It's actually not that ew. There's a lot to be said for all this alternative medicine garbage. Namely that she takes me out for Strawberry Dream Donuts after."

"You have a seriously sweet tooth."

"Sweet tooth, sweet heart." She hugged me and pushed me away and went off laughing.

31

GINGER

Flip started shaking when we were two blocks away, and then I heard them—Jeanie and Leo—from two houses up the block. I didn't even go inside. I sat on the stoop. Flip burrowed into my hoodie pocket.

"You think the poor kid wants to be here either?" Aunt Jeanie said. "Nobody wanted it to be this way. He's my sister's kid."

"Ex*actly,*" Leo said. "He was Tess's, not yours."

"He is, though. He's my responsibility. I promised."

"He thinks I'm a loser. He looks down on me. It's enough to make me want to start drinking again."

"No way, Leo. Uh-uh. You're not going to get away with that."

"With what?"

"Blaming Ben for your lack of self-control."

"It's *not* a lack of self-control. I can't help myself. It's a disease."

"Whatever it is, it isn't Ben's fault."

"The dog too. It's all too much. Too many moving parts. I like it simple."

"Everybody does, Leo. It just isn't, okay? When are you going to grow up?"

"We never used to be like this, babe. We never used to fight."

"Sure we did."

"Not like this, honey. Not like this."

I texted Aunt Jeanie.

> BC: My friend and I have a huge science project due tomorrow.
> Can I stay over at his house tonight to finish it up?

A second later Aunt Jeanie and Leo stopped arguing. She told him about my text. "Do you think Tess would let him sleep over at a friend's on a school night?"

"Are you kidding?" Leo said. "A night off. This is a gift."

Flip stopped shaking the second we turned the corner. My phone pinged with a text from Aunt Jeanie.

> JC: No problem. Good luck.

"I lost my key," I said.

"Where's your aunt?" Mrs. Mold said, pulling me inside the house. Flip trotted up to Ginger the cat and let her lick his ears. One of the girls fed him ice cream from her spoon.

"Mexico," I said. "They're on vacation."

"Coffin, I'm the mother of seven children. I can tell when

I'm not getting the truth. Eight children. When are they coming back from Mexico?"

"They'll be home late tonight, Mrs. Mold, I swear."

Chucky and I settled in to watch *Spider-Man*. One of the older girls ran in with a laptop and showed me a deodorant commercial from probably twenty years ago. The pretty woman sniffs her pits and dances around the kitchen and rose petals fall and birds sing. "It's Mommy," the girl said. "Wasn't she an awesome actress? You totally believe she smells terrific, right?"

"Charice, get out," Chucky said.

"I'm Charmaine."

"Whatever. Coffin, did you hear the latest about Rayburn?"

"Do I want to?"

"His mom threw him out. He's living at his cousin's, and the cousin's in the Mafia and he's killed like a thousand people and he's been to jail. You know that completely trashed house by the train station? That's where his cousin is. I give Rayburn a week before he gets locked up too."

"How do you know these things?"

"I like gossip and Angelina likes people to feel sorry for her, like woe is me, my idiot boyfriend's in trouble again, isn't life so unfair? Dude, I can't believe you feel bad for him."

"I didn't say that."

"You didn't have to."

"I better get to bed."

"We're not even halfway into the movie," Chucky said.

"I already saw it like ten times."

"So?"

Mrs. Mold gave me a Benadryl—a second one—and set me up on the couch in the basement. It was nice and quiet down there. I wondered if I could make myself like Leo. He wasn't that bad. Yes, I could do it. I would. I just needed to catch my breath first, to get a good stress-free night's sleep, to dream about an awesome future: Halley and me and Flip and Read to Rufus and *The Magic Box* and how even if it was only in a made-up story I was on my way to see my mom again, the Contessa of Starlight, and it all started to feel so real.

This really loud wheezy sound woke me just before sunrise. Both dogs were with me on the couch now. So was the cat. Good old Ginger was curled up practically on top of my head. The wheezy sound was me. I fumbled through the dark to find my jeans and my inhaler. It was empty.

32

HOW WAS MEXICO?

The emergency room wasn't too crowded. I heard Aunt Jeanie before I saw her. The clicks from her high heels echoed in the hallway. "I can't possibly thank you enough," she said.

Mrs. Mold waved her off. "Coffin's an angel. How was Mexico?"

Aunt Jeanie cocked her head, and I read her mind: Why are you asking me about a trip I took a year ago? "Bliss," she said. "Have you been?"

"Can't say I have." Mrs. Mold gave me a hard look, then she pecked my forehead. "Well, I'd better get a move on. The Nightgown Nightmares run roughshod over Charles. That's the name of their karaoke band."

Aunt Jeanie filled out the paperwork while I finished inhaling the medicine from the nebulizer. "Stay home and rest," the doctor said. That's the last thing I wanted to do. The medicine made me jumpy. Half an hour later we were in the car. "Can we swing by Chucky's to pick up Flip?"

"I'm prepared," Aunt Jeanie said. The backseat was wrapped in a gray blanket. "Ben, how are you feeling?"

"Better. The medicine always helps."

"No, I mean about everything. You know, living with Leo and me."

"Good."

She looked at me and then back at the road. "I think that was the most unconvincing 'good' imaginable. Come on now. It's just us here. How are you feeling?"

"Like I'm messing you guys up," I said.

She pulled the car over and held my hand for a little bit. "I can't have you feel that way, okay?"

"Okay."

"It's going to take some time."

"I know."

"I feel awful for you."

"I don't want you to, though."

"I want to help you. Leo does too. We're all adjusting. It's a learning curve, right? I'm completely thrown, Ben. Tess was so easy about everything. The worst things could happen, and she smiled right through them. I miss her so much, you know?"

"I know."

"I looked up to her. I wanted to be her. But I couldn't. She was always so pie in the sky, and for me it was always, I better have the raincoat handy. I don't want that to be true, but it is. *I'm* messing *you* up."

"No. You got stuck with me."

"Will you stop *saying* that? Please, all right? I'm going to be better. I promise. We'll keep each other's spirits up, okay? You and me. And Leo too. We're all still reeling, right? Things will get better. We just need time to pass. It'll work out fine. I really think it will."

"Okay," I said. "Okay. It'll work out."

"Yes." She wiped her eyes and got herself together. "We'll get the dog now, and then I'll make you some homemade soup. I'd very much like to do that for you. Now, connect your phone to the stereo and play me your favorite music."

I played her this rap ballad Mom loved, full of banjos and trumpets that got her singing along and up out of her chair and dancing, and she'd get me going too, and we swung each other around. The chorus went:

What's your worry, what's your hurry,

where you running off to?

Stay a while, dance up a smile,

remember we're free to be true.

We're free. We're always. We're you and me.

I was so happy remembering her, the way Mom laughed loud when she danced like that, and then I looked over to Jeanie and she was crying again.

33

THE MYSTICAL MANHATTAN
BOOKSTORE TOUR

Leo was still asleep when Aunt Jeanie and I got back to
Cypress Hills. "Poor guy was up all night packing boxes for
an early UPS pickup," Aunt Jeanie said.

"Mine are ready to go too," I said. "My books, I mean."

"Fabulous. We'll drive them to Strand as soon as you're
feeling better."

"I feel terrific, really," I said.

"No, rest. Soup's on the way."

I sat out on the back porch with Flip. The fake marble
angel had arrived. Its face was—shocker alert—weepy. I
called Halley. *"Why are you home on a school day?"* she
said.

I told her, and she wanted to bring me chocolate-covered
pretzels. "I can't sit still," I said. "Let's go into the city."

~~~

The Mercurious-mobile pulled up to the house. We loaded the book boxes into it. "Ben, are you sure you're up for all this activity?" Aunt Jeanie said.

I felt like dancing. Halley's wig that day was gold with pink leopard spots. Leo came outside with some serious bed head. Mercurious put out his hand. "Mike Lorentz."

"Right, right. Leo Petit." He wiped his hand on his sweat shorts and shook. "I would have done this. Driven Ben, I mean, to the bookstore. I feel bad now. Can I get you a beer? Actually, I, we're out of beer. We have plenty of coffee, though."

"I think the sellback desk closes at one," I said. I had no idea when the sellback desk closed.

"I see," Leo said. "I see. Well, thanks, Mark. Thanks for helping out champ here, I guess."

"I'd love to take you up on that drink another time, Leo," Mercurious said. "We all should get together for dinner."

"That sounds nice," Aunt Jeanie said.

Mercurious helped us load the books into Strand, and then he was off to the Museum of Natural History to talk with the parents of this kid who was having his bar mitzvah party there the next week. The clerk opened the boxes. "You took good care of these," he said. "We'll have an estimate for you by five or so."

We went to Mickey D's and got shakes and a burger for Flip. Halley only had two sips and gave me the rest of her shake, and I was completely messed up with a sugar rush. "Okay, so how's this for the next installment of *The Magic Box*?" I said. "Flip pilots the golden blimp toward the moon Libris without incident."

"He's an expert guide dog, duh." She took back her milk shake and gave some to Flip. His head disappeared into the cup.

"Flip docks the blimp to the antenna on top of the Branch for Interstellar Travel, where Penny is waiting with a dish of Chips Ahoy! of course."

"How much do you love my mom? She's the total Queen of Cookies."

"She whisks Helen, Bruce, and Flip into the star map room and rolls out a chart that goes from one end of the library to the other. Flip trots over it, sniffing one route and then another, until he finds the one he wants and marks it off with two scratches that make an X. Penny looks really worried. 'Flip has chosen the fastest route, but also the most dangerous,' Penny says. Turns out the route goes smack-dab through the Rayburn Belt."

"It has to be done," Halley said. "'However,' Penny says, 'I'm less worried about the nefarious warlock zombie overlord Rayburn than I am the danger you present to yourselves. Promise me you won't peek into the magic box until you get to Mundum Nostrum.'"

"It's that scary, what's inside?" I said.

"That *powerful*."

"Wow."

"Totally."

The manager came over. "Excuse me, kids, but you can't have the dog in here."

"He's a therapy dog," Halley said.

"It's okay," I said. "We'll go."

We went out. "You need to stand up for your rights," Halley said, "not to mention Flip's."

"Let's do a bookstore tour," I said. "Book people love dogs."

"We're selling back all your books and now you want to buy new ones. This makes perfect sense."

"Me and my mom used to do like four a Saturday."

"Let's start at McNally Jackson," Halley said. "It's mystical in there."

"Mystical?"

"The air's buzzy, like when you're watching a lightning storm that's far away and can't hurt you but it lights up the whole sky pink with violet curls." We went to the sci-fi section and sat on the floor, back-to-back, and read while this little boy pet Flip.

"Ha, I got you to like *I, Robot*," I said.

"It's purely research for *The Magic Box*," Halley said. "This is the price I pay for having a writing partner with spectacularly undeveloped reading tastes."

Next we went to Broadway, to the Scholastic bookstore. There was a huge painting of Clifford the Big Red Dog. Flip whined to climb out of the backpack. At Books of Wonder, Peter, the guy who ran it, knew both of us. "And I often thought you should know each other," he said. "When it comes to book lovers, destiny is reality." He treated us to snacks at the Birdbath Bakery. Halley had two bites of chocolate muffin and gave me the rest. At Barnes & Noble Union Square she bought her dad sparkly purple reading glasses. The last stop was Housing Works. "Everybody who works here's a volunteer," Halley said. "They give all the money to people who are HIV positive or have AIDS, and especially to those who're homeless. Ben, we're so lucky."

"That's what Mom used to say. This was her favorite." We went to the checkout desk. "Coffin for a pickup," I said to the clerk. I'd called it in the week before.

"Let me guess," Halley said. "*Star Wars IV, A New Hope*, to replace the *three* copies we just dropped off at Strand."

The clerk handed me *Feathers*. I handed it to Halley. Her eyes widened on the yellow sticker on the cover: SIGNED COPY.

Halley Lorentz screamed so loud the store went quiet. "OMG! *She* held this book. *I'm* holding this book. It's like I'm holding Jacqueline Woodson's hand! Flip, total knuckle bump! Ben Coffin, you are the most seriously amazing human being ever!" We went to the café and took turns reading parts we liked, and then she got to the line about the special moments. "'Moments that stay with us forever and ever.' And there's that face again," she said.

"That's the one line I don't like," I said.

"Of course you do."

"It's a lie. You can't go back."

"But *The Magic Box*, the time travel to the past—"

"Is a story, fantasy. I'm talking about science now. Everything vanishes. It has to. That's how time works. My mom's gone, okay? The sooner I accept that, the fact I'll never see her again, the sooner I can move on."

"You can see her every time you close your eyes and think about her."

"But she's not *there*. Not *here*. She's ashes under a fake marble angel in a little yard in Cyprus Hills. That's it. That's all that's left of her."

"No. Please. I can't think that way. I can't have *you* think that way. I really, *really* need you to believe that we're forever." Her face was scrunched and red and wet.

She was freaking me out. One minute she's laughing and the next she's crying like somebody died. That's when it hit me. You don't tell a friend who's between chemotherapy treatments that you don't believe life goes on forever somehow, some impossible, non-scientific way. No, you be a good friend, and you lie. "Look, I wasn't thinking right," I said. "I was feeling sorry for myself and got messed up there for a second. Truth told, I *do* believe. Halley, seriously, I do."

"You don't, though. You don't." She held Flip close, and he licked her eyes. She put him in my lap and got up. "I better head on home."

"Sure, no problem. Let's go."

"Alone, Ben. I need to think, okay?"

"Halley—"

"No." She put her hands on my chest to stop me from following her. An old guy said to her, "Is he bothering you?"

She got on the bus and pushed into the crowd and I couldn't see her anymore.

34
THE DUMBEST THING
I EVER DID

I called but she wouldn't answer. I texted her and got nothing back. Now I really understood how she felt when I didn't reply to the texts she sent those days leading up to my mom's funeral. Then my phone did beep. It was Strand.

The store was crowded now, and I felt a little dizzy waiting on line to pick up the money. Flip yipped at me and put up his paw and cocked his head. He did a little dance that made everybody laugh, except me. When it was my turn at the counter, the man handed me six hundred dollars. "We gave you top price, I promise," the guy said. "The books were in excellent shape overall. You averaged around a dollar fifty each. You had just about four hundred volumes there. What, you think they were worth more?"

"No, the money's great," I said. "Thanks. It's a lot more than I thought I'd get."

"Then why do you look so . . . ?"

"So what?"

"Like somebody just socked you in the face?"

I was so messed up, I took the wrong train, my old one, to where I used to live. I didn't realize my mistake until the last stop when everybody got off. I got off too. I needed to walk around outside where there was more light.

Flip and I went to the boardwalk. His tail wasn't up and wagging the way it usually would be on a nice day, when we were walking by the beach. My sadness was getting into him. This man in a wheelchair was coming from the other direction. He had two beggars cups and no legs. He was telling me some story about why he needed money, but I wasn't really listening. I was too busy staring into his eyes. He looked really familiar, but I just couldn't figure out from where. I gave him fifty bucks. That was how the guy at Strand paid me, all fifty-dollar bills.

The man in the wheelchair looked at the bill, then he looked at me, and then he looked up to the sky and howled and said, "Woohoo!" He did a wheelie and spun around and said to anybody who'd listen, "Now *this* kid is an angel! Seriously. This kid has true power. This young man *understands*, okay? He has wisdom. Man, you're a gift, okay? You and that beautiful dog. You made my day, little brother. You made my day. It's not the money, I swear. It's your heart. Bless you.

This is everything, man. This is everything." That's when I knew who he reminded me of. Mom. Same eyes, filled with laughing, even during sad times, when she made me give that crummy old dollar to the woman who had sold Flip. I'd said it was nothing, just a lousy buck, but she made me look into her eyes and hear her when she said it was everything.

This man in the wheelchair was a magician for sure. He made me feel like maybe my mom's spirit was still around, traces of her. He made me feel good. Flip too. His tail was up and whipping around. I needed to keep feeling this way, that maybe the beautiful moments in your life, the people you love really can live forever. All you have to do is remember them, like Halley said.

I found somebody else on Neptune Avenue, an old woman pushing a shopping cart full of blankets and a ripped plastic bag filled with clothes. She didn't flip out like the man in the wheelchair when I gave her fifty dollars, but she was just as happy, I'm pretty sure. She was missing teeth, but she smiled like she didn't care. Her laugh was pretty, like a song you can dance to.

A woman in the deli was going to have to put some food back because she didn't have enough money, until I gave her fifty dollars.

The hot dog vendor in front of the aquarium didn't have any business and looked pretty hopeless until I bought franks for me and Flip and told him to keep the change.

I'd given away all but one of the fifty-dollar bills. I figured I'd keep the last one and put it with the money I was saving up from my coupon deliveries, for when I turned sixteen and I could live on my own.

Except I wouldn't be following Halley up to college anymore. All that lightness I'd felt that last half hour, giving away the money, was gone now.

I was about to get back onto the train when I remembered what Chucky told me, that Rayburn was living just down the street with his cousin. I turned around to look back to the end of the block. "What do you think, Flip?"

Flip cocked his head.

The house was even worse than Chucky said. It was more than beat-up. Half the windows were broken. The little front yard was weeds and garbage. Flip looked at me like, Are you sure you want to do this?

I went to the door and knocked. This guy with slicked hair and no shirt answered, even though it wasn't warm that day. There weren't any lights on in the house, and sheets over the window blocked out the sun. The house smelled like rotten food. The guy nodded, like, What do *you* want?

"Damon around?"

"Damon!"

Rayburn was squinting when he came to the door. The

sun was low and bright in his eyes. He rubbed them, like he couldn't believe it was me. "Coffin?"

He looked bad. Really bad. He looked smaller than I remembered, shorter, thinner—and dirty. His hair was all greasy. I gave him that last fifty-dollar bill, knowing the second the money left my hand that it wouldn't feel anything like it did when I gave away the other bills.

He looked at the bill, then at me. "What's your problem, man?" he said. "What are you doing here?"

When I was walking up the steps to the house, I was thinking that if there was a heaven, and my mom was looking down, she would be proud of me. But now she just felt so far away. It all felt bad now, even when I gave away the other fifty-dollar bills, like I'd bought people into being happy, into making me feel good. Still, I gave it a shot with Rayburn. "I heard you were having a hard time," I said. I headed down the steps.

His cousin came out and said, "What's up? Problem out here?"

"Dude just gave me fifty bucks," Rayburn said.

"Why?"

"That's what I said."

"Maybe he's got a crush on you. That little dog, man. That's a girl's dog. Hey, why'd you give my boy Damon fifty bucks?"

I was moving faster now, heading for the front gate. It

was lopsided and dragged on the concrete and hard to open. Another guy was out there now, also no shirt, lots of tattoos. They started calling me names, I probably don't have to say which ones. One of the guys threw half a sandwich at me. Flip and I ran, and they were laughing really loud now. I looked back over my shoulder, and Rayburn was laughing too. He couldn't look weak in front of his boys. He cursed me, but his heart wasn't in it, I could tell. His eyes were wet, like he was going to cry. He looked mad, then sad for a second, then mad again, like he remembered he wasn't allowed to be nice. I was mad too. Mad at myself. How could I be so stupid? I really was losing it. Losing everything, my mind, my money. Losing everyone.

35
THE FAKE MARBLE ANGEL

I saw Leo from outside the house. He was on the phone, pacing in the kitchen. I didn't bother to go in. I took the alleyway into the backyard and sat on the rock next to the fake marble angel. Her eyes had no pupils, I noticed now. Leo came out. His shirt and shorts were all sweaty. "Went for a run," he said.

I nodded.

"Jeanie's still out there," he said. "Yeah. So how'd you do? You make out okay with the books? You didn't let them rip you off, did you?"

"They paid me fine."

"Good. A man makes money, right? Attaboy." He slapped my back as he walked past me. He bent to pull a weed from a crack in the patio. Flip slinked away from him, toward me. Leo stood up and turned toward the weed bucket right when Flip was sneaking behind him. Leo stepped on Flip's foot, Flip yelped. Leo hopped to get off Flip's paw and tripped over a crack in the concrete. He put out his hands to break his fall, but like I said, Leo was a big guy. He landed hard and cursed. "I think he broke my wrist," he said. I tried to help him up but he pulled away. "Get off me," he said. He looked at his wrist. "If it's broken, I'm gonna be mad."

"I'm sorry, Leo," I said.

"Really mad." His eyes landed on Flip. "Stupid dog!" Then he kicked Flip—hard too. Very hard. Hard enough that Flip flew from where Leo kicked him, into the fence. Flip yelped and then staggered and sat and panted and whimpered. He was shivering when I picked him up.

"I can't believe you just did that."

"Stupid little rat!"

"He didn't mean it," I said.

"You can't train him not to be in the way all the time?"

"He weighs like ten pounds," I said. "You could have killed him."

"Stop with the drama, will ya? He's *fine.* Look at him. Freakin' dog." He rotated his wrist. "Ah that kills. Yeah, I think it's broken."

"You wouldn't be able to move it around like that if it was," I said.

"Excuse me, what'd you say?"

"Freaking idiot."

"*What?*"

"Nothing."

"Where do you get it into your head that you can speak to

me that way? I open my house to you, and this is how you talk to me?"

"I said I was sorry, okay?"

"No, not okay. What'd you just call me?"

"It slipped."

"Let it slip again. I need to hear it, just to be sure I heard what I think I heard. Hey, I'm talking to you!"

Him being so mad, well, it got me even madder. I practically yelled it. "I said you're an *idiot*."

And that's when it happened. Leo swung out at me with a big, meaty, open hand, the one connected to his supposedly broken wrist. He slapped me across my face hard enough to make my head whip to the side. My cheek stung and then went numb. Everything got really still, really quiet. The only thing I heard was the birds. A crow, I think, across the street in the park, and then maybe a sparrow or whatever it was, tweeting high-pitched.

I guess his wrist really wasn't broken. He wasn't rubbing it anymore. He ran his hands through his hair, pulling at it a little. He looked scared. Maybe as scared as I was. All I had to do was call the cops, and they'd pull me out of there fast. Yup, I'd be on my way to foster care. That was the problem: They didn't let you bring pets into the foster homes. Flip would be taken to the dog pound. He buried his head in my armpit and trembled so bad I thought he was having a seizure.

I scooped up the dog carrier backpack and went into the

house, into my room, and got my money sock, which had nine dollars in it because I gave the rest to Aunt Jeanie to put in the bank for me. I grabbed the little picture of me and Mom from the beach that day. I was trying to stuff the bigger one of Laura into the backpack when Leo came in.

"Champ," he said.

I grabbed Flip and the backpack and pushed past Leo and ran, but I had to go back to get my stupid inhaler. Leo was following me around, desperate. He kept saying, "Champ, please, we have to talk about this. Hang on just a minute now," and you bet I didn't. Flip and I were *gone.*

36

THE MOBILE MOTEL

The texts started coming in from Aunt Jeanie. Please come back *to the house*. We're waiting for you *at the house*. We'll be *in the house* expecting your call. She never used the word *home*. I checked for a text from Halley. Nope. I disabled my location tracking. This hacker kid in one of the foster homes taught us how to do it. He was always running away, and he was good at staying hidden until he ran out of money or got sick. The cops were definitely going to try to trace me when Aunt Jeanie called them, which eventually she would have to. That's when Leo would have to tell her he hit me. I didn't want him to go to jail or anything, but no way was I going back there. No way. What a mess.

The sun set, and the air up by the park got cold fast. Flip and I got on the bus, and I held him too close, even though he didn't try to squirm away. I was shaking really bad, and that got him shaking worse. I tried to stop thinking about how I couldn't do anything right, that maybe it was good

Mom wasn't around anymore. This way she wouldn't see how bad I messed everything up—and everyone, Jeanie and Leo, Halley most of all.

I was so freaked, I started to wheeze. I had to take three shots off my inhaler. It was hard to hold the medicine in my lungs, like you're supposed to for a few seconds, before you breathe it out, because I was crying, like the kind of crying where you're so panicked that your heart is beating faster than when you're sprinting. Except you're not sprinting. You're just sitting there, realizing, seeing your life for what it really is, a mistake. It had to be, feeling so bad like this. That's when it all started to hit me, that Mom was dead. I mean, I knew she was gone, but now I *really* knew. She was in fact totally and absolutely nowhere, Tess Coffin. Because if she was *some*where, she wouldn't let me and Flip be in such a bad way. Somewhere like an intersecting dimension, where maybe she could whisper the right words into my mind and tell me what to do. I'd felt lost at some of the foster homes I was in, but never like this. Now I had zero protection, and worse than that, how the heck was I supposed to keep Flip safe? I just didn't know where to go.

I clicked up a video of Mom. She was in the supermarket, trying all the cheese samples, acting all fancy with a fake British accent. *"Now this one has a* weighty *flavor. Do try one, luvvy."* And she got that sad old lady in the hairnet to crack half a smile. Then I clicked through pictures of Halley and me, selfies she took and texted to me, and our foreheads are touching, and Flip's in every one of them. And then I stopped looking. I shut my eyelids so tight they hurt. I tucked Flip inside my hoodie, and pretty quickly he stopped shivering and poked his head out from the hood and licked my neck.

Somebody shook my shoulder. The bus driver. The bus was pulled over and empty. "It's midnight," she said. She was holding Flip. "He had to pee. I took him out."

"Sorry," I said.

"Lucky it was me and not somebody else. They would have taken him out and kept right on going with him. He know any tricks?"

"Flip, surf."

He surfed her lap and kissed her. "I want you to sit up close, by me," she said. "It's very late. I'm supposed to call the police, but I won't."

"I'm—"

"I know," she said. "I know." She gave me half of a foot-long hero from Subway. I shared the turkey with Flip. She had a bottle of water for me too, and Flip lapped it up from my palm. She put her hand on my forehead and said, "I know," and then she got back to driving. The city passed by the windows. All the lights. The people in the windows of the apartment buildings just doing normal stuff, watching TV, cooking. The people in cars. They all seemed to be leaning forward a little too much. Time slowed down until I thought it just might stop for real. If I didn't have Flip to take care of, I wouldn't have cared if I lived or died, and I was sure nobody else would have either, not really, not anymore.

At one a.m. another driver came on board. The nice driver talked softly to him. She pointed to the left side of her face, the same side where Leo slapped me. The other driver kept shaking his head. He took out his phone, and that's when I got off the bus, and Flip and I ran. When we were clear of the bus I stopped to look at my face in a car window. It wasn't that bad. My lip was a little puffy, and you could see red where his hand went across my cheek—nothing too crazy. In a day or so it'd all be gone. Except it would never be gone, not for Leo either probably.

We went to the Long Island Rail Road waiting room. It was big and I remembered from the times when me and Mom took the train back to Brooklyn from the mall that lots of people slept there. I figured Flip and I would be safe enough until I could figure out what to do, but I couldn't and we weren't. Some creep sat next to me. "You hungry?"

"No."

"I see. Sure. Then maybe you need a place to stay tonight?"

"*No.*" I looked for a cop, and then I remembered I couldn't let one see me.

The creep smiled and nodded. "I like your dog. May I pet it?"

I tucked Flip under my arm and got out of there, and the guy followed and kept saying, "Wait. Hey, wait," and I ran. Yup, Mom was dead for sure.

37

FLIP'S EYES
AND THE LAST GOOD-BYE

I went up the Molds' porch steps and sat on the top one and put Flip in my lap so we could see into each other's eyes. I saw my reflection in his, and I was all warped. "You'll be safe here, boy. That's all I want, even if I can't be with you. You'll be happy." It was cold and he was trembling so bad now. I hugged him one last time and tied him to the door. He cocked his head, and I know he was waiting for me to say it. The thing I said every time I dropped him off at the Molds'. That I was coming back. That I promised. I turned away fast, and he barked, and I ran to the corner and called Chucky.

"Coffin, what the freak? You know what time it is?"

"Chucky, you hear Flip, right? He's downstairs. Let him in. Bye."

"Ben, wait—"

I did wait too, until he came down and picked up my dog.

He looked around the street, but I was hidden pretty good between the cars. Flip saw me, though. His eyes were on me and he was barking like crazy as Mold brought him in.

I went around the corner and puked and sank down against the side of a building behind a stupid dumpster again. My head ached. I just needed to close my eyes for a minute and catch my breath, except I fell asleep.

38
THE WORST TIME
TO GET THE FLU

It was hot when I woke up, way too hot for fall. It was like in
the middle of summer. The street stank from all the garbage
bags out at the curb. The sun wasn't too high yet, but the
air was like it got late in the afternoon, no breeze. The sun-
light was way too bright. Everything glowed mean. I pushed
myself up from behind the dumpster and went to the corner.
I peeked around it to see the Mold house. The curtains were
pulled back, but nothing was happening in the windows. The
avenue was busy with school buses and delivery trucks rushing around—the traffic was loud, lots of horns and sirens.

I waited until Mrs. Mold came out with one of the girls. She
put her on the bus. Flip came out and slumped down on the
porch. Mrs. Mold limped up the porch steps and sat and pet
Flip. His tail flicked a little. He'd be okay in a few days, I was
pretty sure. That made me feel good, and good and lonely too.
Mrs. Mold scooped him up and kissed him and took him in.

My stomach twisted up again. I didn't puke this time. I had to eat. I went up the avenue to Dunkin' Donuts and got a sandwich and iced tea, and after that I only had four dollars left. The lady at the counter was looking at me weird. "You okay?"

"Yeah, why?"

She gave me a hot tea with lemon and a bunch of napkins. "Clean yourself up. Your nose is running."

How could I have a cold on such a hot day? But she was right. My nose was a mess. I was shivering a little too, and the air conditioner made it worse. I went out to the street and looked for a quiet place to eat. It must have been a hundred degrees out there. I caught sight of myself in a store window. I looked rough, like I'd slept outside, which of course I did. My hair was greasy and plastered to my head, and my clothes were grimy and wrinkled and soaked with sweat. One of my eyes was pink and puffy the way it can get when you have a fever. It would pass. I didn't get sick often, and if I did, it was never that bad, or this bad. I stopped to take a bite of sandwich but, even though I was starving, the thought of eating made me want to hurl. I walked for a while, and I kept bumping into people. I was having a hard time keeping my head up. I made my way to the boardwalk, to our spot—mine and Halley's and Flip's—except it wasn't our spot anymore. An old man was sleeping on the bench. Luna Park was stock-still, empty. The beach was empty too, with everybody at work and school, I figured.

I went down to the sand and sat in the shade under the boardwalk. Boy, I was really shivering now. I couldn't even get myself to nibble the sandwich crust. The smell of it made me retch. Yup, I was sick for sure—the kind of sick you can't cure on your own. The kind you need to go to a doctor for. I fed the sandwich to the seagulls, and then I curled into myself and hoped nobody found me before I died, because then they would call the cops, and they would take me to the hospital and I'd get better, and then what would I do? Where would I go? I didn't want to be anywhere anymore. Not without Flip. Without Halley.

Except suddenly I wasn't without Halley. She was shaking my shoulder. "Get up, Coffin." She looked awesome, like she did the first time I met her, way back nine months ago, over winter break. Her wig this morning looked like her real hair, long and loopy, light brown. She was kind of tanned too. She held my hand and her fingers were nice and warm.

"How'd you find me?" I said.

"I'm always keeping an eye out for you. Hey? You can't give up. We have to finish our novella."

"We're friends again?"

"Like we ever weren't? I have to make sure you get to see what's inside the magic box, right? The Greatest Treasure. You're so close to figuring it out, Ben. You just have to keep going. It's right around the corner. We have to get you all better. The Read to Rufus kids are depending on us. We can't leave Brian hanging. Right, Mom?"

"You'll break his heart, Ben," Mrs. Lorentz said, hurrying up to us. "Mine too. You poor baby. Come here, sweetheart. Let me check your temperature." She brushed back my hair and kissed my forehead and said, "You're burning up. Here, let me hold you." She hugged me and held me the way she did at Rosh Hashanah, when she didn't let go. She rocked me a little and hummed some lullaby or other, the way Mom did that one time when I got sick last winter. Halley joined in too, hugging and humming. There we were, the three of us, in the shadow of the boardwalk, holding each other really tight, and we were safe. The vibrations from their humming went into me, and I felt buzzy and better, and I would have smiled if I didn't feel so bad about Flip. "He'll be mad I gave him up," I said.

"Oh, he could never be mad at you, Ben," Mrs. Lorentz said. "He loves you no matter what. Look."

Flip was pawing at my leg, begging me to scoop him up. "I've never seen his tail wag so fast," I said. "I don't even think that's humanly possible, right? Not humanly. You know what I mean."

But they didn't. They couldn't. Halley and Mrs. Lorentz were gone. The waves were frozen still. There wasn't any movement anywhere—the seagulls hung midair, and their wings weren't flapping. They weren't squawking. There was no sound. Nothing. Everything was fading away, the heat, the light, and I was alone, and it was cold and dark and silent, except for one thing, Flip's whimpering. And it wasn't fading either. It was getting louder. So loud I could have sworn that little mutt was crying right in my ear.

I woke up where I'd passed out, behind the dumpster. Flip crawled into my armpit, and he was licking my face like I was ice cream. I opened my eyes wide, and it was still night. My phone was buzzing with half a dozen texts from Chucky.

CM: Flip got out. Get back here and help me find him.

I looked around the corner. Flip had dug through that cardboard Dr Pepper box taped to the hole in the peekaboo window that ran alongside the Molds' front door.

I texted Chucky not to worry, that Flip was here with me, and he was. He really was.

39

COUPONS, MOVIES
AND PROMISES

Flip and I went to the all-night McDonald's and split a burger. Then I bought a toothbrush and some water from the all-night drugstore. The people who were out at this hour all looked like me and Flip. They looked suspicious, like they were expecting something bad to happen any old minute now.

I went to where I picked up my coupons and brushed my teeth in the alley. The sun started to come up and Flip and I huddled and waited. My boss showed up in his van. "Earlier than usual today, Coffin. You don't look so good."

"Thanks boss."

"You all right?"

"Could I borrow ten dollars?"

We delivered the coupons, and Flip was his old self, trotting right alongside me, head high. Every time I looked at him, he did a little spin and nipped at my sneaker. Then it was more

McDonald's until the movie theater opened. "Shouldn't you be in school?" the guy at the ticket window said.

"I homeschool."

"They let you watch *Planet of the Apes* for class these days, huh? You have it pretty good."

"Don't I know it," I said. School. It was the last thing on my mind. The bullying, eating lunch under the stairs, Angelina's stupid tricks, gum in the water fountain, Ronda's shoves—they all seemed so *nothing* now, so far away, as far away as the idea of going to college with Halley or going to school at all anymore. I was becoming one of them, the kids who disappeared.

Once I settled into the back of the theater and the lights went down I snuck Flip out of the backpack and he slept inside my hoodie. I set my phone to buzz me awake a little before the movie ended, and then I snuck into another movie and did the same thing, and then another after that, until three o'clock, and then we had to go. Even if Halley wasn't into being friends with me anymore, I wasn't about to let down Mrs. Lorentz. I was going to keep my promise.

40
TRAVELER BRIAN
AND THE TUNNEL OF LIGHT

"Ben, my Ben, what happened to you two?" Mrs. Lorentz said. "Those bags under your eyes. You look like you haven't slept in a month. What's that mark on your cheek?"

"How's Halley?"

"She was up crying all night. You didn't answer my question. That Rayburn character Halley told me about—did he hit you again?"

"It was a stop sign."

She folded her arms and frowned. "A stop sign?"

"I'm so embarrassed. I was looking at my phone while I was walking, and I walked right into the stop sign pole." I saw somebody do that once. "Aren't they waiting for us upstairs?"

They were too, the whole Read to Rufus gang, everybody except Halley. Flip gave out knuckle bumps and jumped up into Brian's lap. I had to keep this going, Flip and Read to

Rufus. It was the only thing that felt good now. The only thing that felt right. "What story are you going to read to Flip today, Bri?" I said.

"I forgot to pick one."

I reached into my backpack. It was my last book, the one Halley had left on the table at Housing Works.

"Fee, *Feathers*?" Brian said.

"You're awesome. This is another one where the ending is sad but happy."

"I better read it to Flip, then," Brian said. "He's waiting for me." And Brian read about the moments that last forever and ever. Hearing the words I almost felt like Halley was reading them to me the way she did the day before at Housing Works, when she was holding my hand.

And then suddenly she was. She was there, and not in a dream. She was a real-life angel this time. She sat next to me and rested her head on my shoulder and listened. She was wearing a soft gray beret, and it felt nice on my cheek. Everything felt perfect in that moment, being there with her and the kids and Mrs. Lorentz and Flip. I was so happy, I didn't worry about the future. It wasn't even on my mind.

We said good-bye to everybody, and then Mrs. Lorentz scooped up Flip and went downstairs to leave Halley and me alone. We hunkered in the safety of the nook behind the Dragonbreath bookcase. "I'm sorry," we both said at the same time. "Let's go walk Flip on the boardwalk and work on *The Magic Box*," I said.

"Can't, stupid doctor's appointment again. Text me tonight, after homework. We can work on it then."

"Thanks," I said.

"For what?"

"Not firing me."

I helped Mrs. Lorentz close up the library, sort of. I disabled the alarm to the alley door and left it unlocked. "You really do look pale, Ben. Here, take this for the ride home." She gave me an orange and a trail mix bar. "How are things back home anyway?"

"You know, settling in."

"Good," her mouth said, but her eyes said, I'm not even close to believing you.

"I better get back to the house for dinner," I said, before she could ask me any more questions.

"Watch those stop signs," she said.

"Yeah," I said, stumbling into the door frame on the way out, pretending to smack my face on it.

"My poor baby," Mrs. Lorentz said. "Let me see."

"I'm fine, I'm fine," I said. "Thanks." I headed for the train, faking like I was a little dazed. If I survived being a teenager, I was thinking I might have a shot at an acting career.

I waited behind the candy stand on the corner until she

left, and then I went into the alley and snuck back into the library. We were alone, me and Flip. We were safe. I read bits of lots of books. I think if there's a heaven it'll be my own private library. I walked along row after row of books and dragged my fingertips over their spines. In the twilight I felt the magic in them. They whispered to me, *Pick me. Do you want to know an awesome secret?*

When the sun was gone for good I read by my phone light. No way was I turning on the lights. The streetlights lit up part of the first floor, and I went there and stared into the silkscreened picture of the old Luna Park parachute tower that rose up from the young adult section. I swear I heard the screams and laughter of the people on the ride.

I had two tins of dog food in the backpack, and it actually didn't taste that bad. I found unopened ketchup packets in the garbage and added hot water from the sink. It warmed me up. I checked my phone and ignored the stream of texts from Aunt Jeanie until I couldn't anymore. She was worried sick. She called the school. Mrs. Pinto called the police. They were so mad at themselves, Leo and Jeanie, she said. Why didn't she think to get the number of the nice woman who took me to the hospital after I had that asthma attack? Please, please, please call *the house.* I texted her, *I'm ok. I need time to think. I feel so bad I'm worrying you. I'll call you when I figure things out.* I thought about what else to say, but I couldn't think of anything except I love you, and

I knew that would just make her uncomfortable. I blocked her after that, because I really didn't think I could stand to read all the sadness she was about to text my way. I was okay there in the library that night. I was with Flip, and I felt like we were really safe there, and I didn't want to be bummed out. I texted Halley.

BC: How was it at the doctor's?

HL: Just a blood test. Next chapter of The Magic Box?

BC: OK. Rayburn has secretly boarded our spaceship, The Golden Tower of Light.

HL: I knew it! The dreaded Rayburn! And?

BC: Flip sniffed him out. He caught Rayburn in the storage bay, where he was trying to steal the magic box.

HL: Yay Flip! Rayburn runs to the airlock where he docked his sneaky invisible ship. If Bruce and Helen don't let him take the box, he's going to whip out his laser sword and cut a hole in the window, and the release of air pressure will blow apart our ship of golden light and everything in it. Do they let him go?

BC: They can't. They need to get that magic box to Tess. Helen tells Rayburn, "Wait! You need the key!" Rayburn checks the lock, and he's laughing, cackling. The box was never locked at all!

HL: Uh, NO, you sneak. Mercurious locked it with the key made of sparks!

BC: He only pretended to! He wanted Helen and Bruce to be able to get to the magic and save themselves in case things got really bad, LIKE NOW. It's like he said, a truly great magician can never keep his magic secret. It's meant to be shared. So once and for all, what's inside the freaking box?

HL: Ask Rayburn. He's opening it!

I waited for her to keep going, and waited. Finally I texted, *And?!*

HL: Rayburn's crying. "This is the Greatest Treasure? OMG it's completely worthless." He totally passes out.

BC: What the freak? What's inside???

HL: Flip snatches the box from Rayburn's hands and sits on it and won't let Bruce and Helen look. Flip's not a biter, but don't push him. Now, how do Bruce and Helen take their revenge on Rayburn? I'll let you handle the gory part.

BC: I say they help him into a spare sleeping pod, pipe some awesome low-key rap into it and tell him to chill until they get to Mundum Nostrum. Once they deliver the magic, Tess will turn him into a half-decent humanoid.

HL: This is why I love you. You know there are no bad guys. OK, awesome story jam session, but—ahem—I didn't get any sleep last night. Must. Go. To. Bed. Gnight. ;0)

"I wish you could read, Flip. I'd ask you if you see what I see. The wink. She sent me the wink. Good joke, right, boy? Yup, ha." I had to look over that last text a few times to be sure it really did say what I though it did. "She actually loves me, Flip—as a friend, I mean, but still." He nipped my nose and did a wiggle worm into my hoodie.

We settled in on a couch in the back office, and I couldn't fall asleep, because I couldn't imagine what was inside that box. I cracked the window to let in some air, and it felt good. I breathed and breathed and breathed a little easier, and then I fell asleep.

I was only asleep a few minutes when Flip's growling woke me. The library was pure dark. The only thing darker was the silhouette of the very tall man standing over me. He drew something from his hip and aimed it at me, and then a thousandth of a second after I heard the click I was hit in the face by a golden tunnel of light.

41

THE MAN WHO COMES
TO TAKE YOU AWAY

"Son, just let me into your phone," the police lady said. The precinct was noisy and crowded, and they had me in a room way at the end of the hall. Hot as it was back there, Flip wouldn't come out from my hoodie pocket. "Tell you what," the cop said. "Just give me your name at least."

"I can't," I said. "We can't go back there."

"Where?"

"Please, just let us go. I'm begging you. We'll be okay, I swear."

"Sweetheart, I'm begging *you*. I only want to help you and your dog, okay? The emergency caseworker is on his way. In about five minutes, he's going to be here. If I don't know your name by then, he takes you away into protective custody. Now, they don't let dogs into the emergency housing facilities."

"I know."

"Your friend there goes to the pound."

"I know. I know. I don't know what to do." Flip kept cocking his head and licking my face.

"Please," she said, "just give me your name."

Somebody leaned into the room and said to her, "There's a guy outside who says he's here to pick him up."

The cop turned to me. "This is your last chance."

"Okay," I said. "Okay. Just promise you'll call Halley and give her my dog."

"Halley?"

"My friend. My best friend."

"Okay. Good. That's a deal. I'll call her. I'll get our little friend here to her myself. And if she doesn't want him, *I'll* take him home. I promise."

"You sure? You have dogs?"

"Two." She showed me a video on her phone. Her dogs were fat and wagging their tails like crazy because she was feeding them cheese puffs. She was my kind of cop.

"Okay, my name is—"

"Ben," somebody said. I looked up and there was Mercurious. He hugged me and told me it was okay, that everything was going to be okay.

42
THE MIDNIGHT MEETING

The clock ticked past midnight and into the month of October. We were sitting around the dining room table. Flip snored belly up in Halley's lap. Mrs. Lorentz ordered pizza but nobody ate. I told them everything—except the part about Leo slapping me. The part about him kicking Flip was enough, though, because when I finished talking, Mrs. Lorentz said, "Okay, you're staying here with us."

"I don't think it's that easy, ma'am," I said.

"Ben, please, I'm a librarian."

"Media specialist," Halley said.

"Either way, stop calling me ma'am."

"It's better than him wanting to send you the wink," Halley said.

I gave Halley *SHUT UP* eyes, and Halley said, "She doesn't even know what it means."

"The emoticon?" Mrs. Lorentz said. "Oh that's so sweet of you, Ben. You send me the wink any old time you want and I'll wink right back. We'll be total wink buddies, how fun!"

Halley gave me a look like, Wow, she's even dopier than you on this one. "You so totally have to stay here with us," she said. "You and Mommers—you two are gonna get along *great*. Yes, it's going to be truly fun to torture you."

"Ben," Mrs. Lorentz said, "I'm thinking you want to call your aunt."

She was going to be a weepy mess. She was going to make me talk to Leo too. I couldn't handle that. My brain was fried. I just needed to pass out. "Can you call her for me?"

"You poor baby. Okay, give me her number. You'll call her tomorrow."

Mercurious said, "Ben, let's get you and Flip set up for bed."

The couch in Mercurious's little home office folded out into a bed. Pictures of stars and galaxies covered the walls. Model planets and airplanes hung from the ceiling, and books were jammed every which way into their cases. He pulled a sparkly blanket off a model of a city, Luna Park 1905. *Dreamland at Night.* It was half built, but the golden tower was almost done. He'd strung miniature lights from the steeple to the smaller towers that surrounded it. The buildings were made of shiny paper. "Turn off the lights," he said. Flip's eyes glowed gold with the reflection. "For her birthday," Mercurious said. "For when she turns fourteen."

43

JEANIE

By the time I was awake the next morning, Mrs. Lorentz had a bunch of papers spread over the dining room table. She and Mercurious were reading through them. Halley was wrapped up in a blanket on the couch. She wore a bright pink wool cap with pink antlers. Flip hopped up into Halley's lap, raised his paw for a knuckle bump, yawned and rolled over for her to scratch his fat little stomach. "I just wish he felt more at home here," Halley said.

"How'd you sleep?" Mercurious said.

"Great," I said. I really did too. I slept so hard I didn't even dream.

"We had a very long talk, your aunt Jeanie and I," Mrs. Lorentz said. "Ben, we need to talk about that *stop sign* you ran into. Look at me. Come here." She held my face to the light to look at where Leo slapped me. There was hardly a mark anymore. I checked myself in the bathroom mirror first thing when I woke up. Mrs. Lorentz frowned. "Does your neck hurt? I need you to be absolutely honest with me."

"I'm okay. Really I am."

"I need to take a picture of your face."

"No, I don't want to make a big thing out of this," I said.

"It is a big thing. It's a very big thing. Hiding it will make it worse."

"It's not like they're ever going to bring another kid into that house. They were okay before I got there. Aunt Jeanie. I don't want to ruin her life."

"You're not. You didn't do anything wrong. The fact that Leo came forward and told Jeanie what happened—that's going to help him a lot. He'll get counseling anyway, and he should. He needs it. You're helping him get the help he needs."

"Doesn't feel that way."

"Ben, you can't go back to that house. Children's Services won't allow it. Now, there's a lot to sort through. I have the social worker coming here in a bit to inspect the apartment. They're running background checks on Michael and me, and we'll know in a few hours if we're going to get the preliminary okay to be foster caregivers. I expect we will. It helps that you and I have known each other for two years. Jeanie is coming over to meet us this afternoon. She only wants you to be happy. And more than anything she wants you to be safe. You're safe here, all right? You're safe with us. All that said, I want you to know that this is not something that can't be undone. You're not trapped here either, if you decide you don't want to stay. After Leo gets whatever counseling he needs, and if he's cleared to be your guardian, you can go back to live with Jeanie if you want to."

"I won't. We won't, me and Flip."

"Mom, seriously?" Halley said. "Why would he want to go back there?"

"I just want you to know your options. We're going to take this one day at a time, Ben, and we're going to follow your lead. Are you okay with that?"

I had to think for a second before I nodded. I wasn't used to calling the shots. I wasn't used to having options. I was almost excited, the way you feel after you see a movie you thought was going to be just okay, but it ended up being great.

Mercurious was looking at me and nodding. Halley cuddled Flip and said, "Everything's gonna be all right, Flip. Everything's gonna be okay."

"So we all agree that Ben is better off living here for the time being?" the social worker said. She turned to Aunt Jeanie. "You're sure you're okay with this?"

Aunt Jeanie was wearing a lot more makeup today. She stared into the center of the table, not at me when she said, "Am I sure, Ben?"

I couldn't get myself to look into her eyes when I nodded.

I looked to Halley instead. She smiled a little sadly and cud-dled Flip.

The social worker showed Jeanie where she had to sign, and she did. She put down the pen. She still wasn't looking at me when she said, "Ben, can you walk me to my car? I have a little something for you."

It was a beautiful afternoon, and now I was glad to get a chance to talk with her. "I just wanted to thank you for everything."

"Stop, Ben," she said. She dabbed her eyes with a cot-ton ball to keep her mascara from running. "I wasn't in the Lorentzes' apartment for even a minute when I knew just how badly I had let you down. Had let Tess down."

"You didn't though."

"I can see why you would rather live with them. They're wonderful. They know how to do it."

"Do what?"

"Halley's spectacular. They did such a beautiful job with her. I just want you to be happy. I'm so sorry. I feel awful about everything. Here, sit in the car with me for a min-ute." We did and she took a small package out of the glove compartment and gave it to me. It was wrapped so perfectly I didn't want to tear the paper. "Save the ribbon," she said. "It's expensive, and you can use it again."

The paper folded away, and it was a framed picture. "I

want you to have this," she said. "It's my favorite of Tess, of the three of us all together."

Mom was in the middle. She had one arm over Jeanie's shoulders and the other over Laura's. They were all laughing, for real too. They wore Santa hats and they might even have been a little tipsy.

"Doesn't she look so beautiful there?" Jeanie said. "She had the loveliest smile, Tess did. Your mother, I mean. Your mom. Ben, can you ever forgive me?"

"For what? You tried to help me."

"That's how he was brought up. Spare the rod and spoil the child. Had I known he would hit you, I would have . . . I don't know. I would have done something to protect you. I've never known him to be violent. He says he's just not cut out to be a parent. Some people aren't. Please don't hate him."

"I don't," I said, which was a lie. Except maybe it wasn't. I don't know. Maybe I felt sorry for him. I definitely didn't like him.

"You're so forgiving. Tess always said you were special. Ridiculously special, is how she put it. I knew you were too, from the little bits of time we got to spend together the last couple of years, but you were good at hiding. You were so quiet. I thought you didn't like me."

"I do though. I do."

"These past few weeks, back at the house, I really wanted

to let you know you I loved you. I just didn't know how. I'm not going to give up, though, okay? I'm going to keep trying. I'm here for you, as much as you want me to be." She hugged me and then pushed me away. "Look at what I did. I got makeup on your shirt."

"It's okay."

"Go, before I start crying. I don't want my mascara to run." It was too late for that. I got out of the car. "Call me tomorrow, all right? Call me and let me know you're okay. We're going to see each other as much as you want, all right? I want to be in on all the beautiful things coming your way. Yes. All the beautiful things." Then she said the last thing as she was driving away. She wasn't looking at me, and her voice was soft, and she said it fast, but she said, "Love you."

I watched her Mercedes get small on the avenue. That car was so clean, and the sun glinted off it, and then it disappeared when she turned the corner. I studied the picture she gave me. Jeanie, Mom and Laura all looked so young. They looked like they weren't worried about anything, like nothing bad could happen, and they would always be this way, laughing, happy, together.

It was such a sunny, breezy day. Sometimes this old woman used to sell flowers on days like this, way down at the other end of the boardwalk. I walked fast down the street toward where she kept her cart. I felt the sun inside me, almost like I was about to float up from the pavement and maybe even fly, so high that I'd be able to see the whole city. The old woman was there, and for five bucks I got the nicest bunch of flowers, reds and purples and pinks. I practically ran home to give them to the Lorentzes. By the time I got back up into their apartment the social worker was gone. Mrs. Lorentz pulled me in for a hug. "I'm so happy you're here," she said. "So grateful." She took the flowers and went to the cabinet for a vase and said, "Go and get your room set up now."

44

CHEWIE

Mercurious had moved all his stuff out of his office into the dining room. I begged him not to, but he did it while I was at school. He left the cool stuff, the pictures of the galaxies, the model planes. I peeked under the sparkly wrap that covered the model of Luna Park 1905 Mercurious was building for Halley's birthday. He'd gotten a little further along. He'd laid down gold foil at the base of the tower and along the beach line. The foil was wrinkled in a pattern to make it look like an ocean filled with quiet little waves.

Above the model was a patch of empty corkboard wall. Mercurious had taken down his diagrams and sketches for the tricks he was working on for that big party he had coming up at the Museum of Natural History. I hung up my Chewie poster. I pushed in the tacks, wondering how long it would be before I had to pull them out again.

Halley came in with Flip and plunked on the bed. She watched me push in the tacks. "So you really are staying then."

"You don't seem too psyched," I said. She looked sad.

"I'm totally psyched. Especially since I have to do another round of chemo next week. It's only once a month, but I feel kind of crummy for a few days after. This way I can make you feel crummy too. I'm messing with you, Coffin. I'm just saying it'll be awesome that you're here. We can cheer each other up."

"How much longer do you have to take the medicine?"

"Not sure. Maybe a few more months, until I'm a hundred and eleven percent. I'll ask the doctor again tomorrow after we get the results from the blood test. That's gonna be one of the best parts about being better. No more bruises on my arms." She showed me the places where they took the blood. The bruises were different colors: yellow, brown, green, purple. She peeled off a Band-Aid, and the bruise there was almost black.

"It's really nice out," I said.

"Let's go to the beach and fly a kite." And that's what we did. It was sparkly purple with a gold tail.

45

THE RAINBOW GIRL
AND THE FLYING TRAPEZE

The next day I was pretty psyched coming home from school, not just because it was Friday but because Halley and I were going to work on *The Magic Box*. I was pretty close to threatening her that if she didn't tell me what was inside it, I wouldn't be friends with her anymore. If it could save a whole planet, the magic had to be something that could spread, like a song that made you feel taller when you heard it. My phone blipped.

Aunt Jeanie. It was a sticker of a cartoon cat waving its paw. I waved back to her with a dopey-looking dog. She wanted to take me to dinner next week. I was sort of afraid to sit down with her. I didn't want to know about Leo, about what was happening with him with the counseling or whatever. I just didn't want to think about him. To remember the way he kicked Flip. But I texted, *Sounds great*.

Halley and Flip were waiting for me on the steps outside the Lorentzes' apartment building. She was smiling but looked tired. She patted the step next to her, and I sat. "Mom's freaking out up there. Mercurious is trying to calm her down. I had to get outside, you know? See what you got yourself into, Coffin? Welcome to the drama."

"What'd I do?"

"Why do you always think it's you?"

"It just usually is, is all."

"Not this time." She took out her phone. The screen was chart after chart of all these numbers in columns with weird headings like *T-Cells* and *Alpha-fetoprotein*.

"What does it mean?" I said.

"It's back. Look, don't freak, because I'm not. I'm totally kicking this thing's butt. I am, Ben."

"You so totally are, I know," I said, but I didn't know anything.

"I knew just now for sure when the doctor called," Halley said, "but I *knew* the day of our bookstore tour. I woke up feeling different that morning. It's like this weird warmth in my lower back."

"Is that how it felt the first time, last winter?"

"No, that time I woke up with blood in my pee and this stomachache that wouldn't go away. I had to go straight into surgery. It was a six-pound tumor. I made the doctor show me a picture of it. I couldn't believe it was inside of me. It looked like a giant's fist, gray with black veins. So look, the chemotherapy I'm going to take this round is a brand-new medicine, and it's a lot stronger, which is awesome, because it's going to completely burn the bad stuff away. It's also going to make me feel pretty sick for a while—like sicker than I'd normally get. I have to start the chemo right away, tomorrow, so I need you to take me to Luna Park today."

"Right now?"

"We'll just bring Flip back upstairs, then we'll go. There's no better time. It's already October, and it'll be closed for the season by the time I'm back to a hundred and eleven percent. I want you to fly with me."

"Fly?"

She grinned. "We need to take a ride on the Boardwalk Flight."

It was basically a mix of skydiving and a slingshot that threw you two hundred feet into the air at a speed of sixty miles an hour. The attendant strapped us into the safety vests. "I probably should have told you, but I'm terrified of heights," Halley said.

"Which is why your heroine from *The Magic Box* is a trapeze artist," I said. "Makes perfect sense."

"It does, if you really think about it," she said. "I might barf all over you."

"This would have been good to know before we got on the ride."

The cable whipped us upward—and backward by our ankles—to the top of the tower. Halley screamed and laughed. "Holy ship, my stomach!"

"Oh boy."

"Do *not* let go of my hand, Ben Coffin!"

"I won't, I promise, even though you're breaking my fingers. Uh-oh, here we go." We swung down toward the boardwalk and then up toward the sun.

"Don't let me fly away! Hold me!"

"I am! I got you!"

"And I got *you*! Ben?"

"Halley?"

"We're flying! We really are! This is so freaking spectacular!" And it was. It was.

46
DON'T BE SCARED

We walked the boardwalk slowly and didn't say anything, and the sun was warm on our faces, and she smiled. She flipped her leg backward to kick me in the butt.

"What was that for?" I said.

"Don't be scared, okay?" she said. "Everything's going to be totally fine."

"I should be saying these things to you," I said.

"But I'm not scared. I swear I'm not. Look." She pointed into the funhouse mirror. It stretched us thin. We were aliens with big eyes and huge heads and we both looked like we were trying really hard not to look scared. Halley aimed her phone at the mirror and took a picture of us. The flash stayed in my eyes that night, especially when I shut them and tried to fall asleep.

Saturday morning breakfast, the four of us held hands. Halley prayed, "God, thank you for this meal. Thank you for us. I hope you get everybody here to see that nobody should stop living the heck out of life the next month or so. Each day is the best day from here on in." She opened her eyes. "Ben, I need you and Flip to keep Read to Rufus going the days I'm not feeling so great. We can't let it fall apart. That's the one thing that will make me mad. Flip, high four." He gave her one and surfed her lap. "Mom, look into his eyes. They're just like Harry's, right?" That was her dog who died. "What's he trying to tell us? Look. You see it, don't you? What *is* that?"

After, I helped Mrs. Lorentz wash the dishes. Out of nowhere she hugged me with wet dish gloves. "I don't know what we would do without you right now."

"She's totally going to beat this thing," I said.

"I know," Mrs. Lorentz said, but she didn't know either.

Flip and I delivered my coupons and met up with Mercurious at the church and watched him finish his magic lesson with the little kids. A girl tripped and cried, "My knee hurts." Mercurious sat her in a chair and sprinkled magic dust on her knee and made her pain vanish. "It works," she said.

"That's right," he said. He patted her head. "All better now."

We got into the sparkly purple SUV and got on the highway. I strapped Flip into the passenger seat, in my lap. "He slept with Halley last night," I said.

"Us too," Mercurious said. "At about three this morning he came scratching at the door."

"Sorry."

"For what? That's his job. Warm everybody up, right?"

We didn't listen to music, we didn't talk. The sky was white, too bright. Halley and her mom had to go earlier so Halley could get a port put into her chest, whatever a port was. Maybe twenty minutes into the ride, Mercurious said, "Ben? Thank you for being here. Without you, this would be unbearable."

47

SIRIUS

I expected more of a hospital-type place. We pulled into a strip mall right off the highway. The waiting room was pictures of horses and forests and this big one of a flower field. "Flip!" Halley said. Her beret that day was fuzzy orange.

Flip surfed and boxed for everybody in the waiting room and hopped into the lap of this little boy who was sitting next to Halley. "Ben, this is Franco. He's awesome."

He was also bald. He kissed Flip and said, "He has bad breath."

"We know," we all said.

The nurse came out. "Okay, Halley, ready to rock?"

Mrs. Lorentz hugged Halley.

"Mom, relax," Halley said.

"I am," Mrs. Lorentz said. "I *am*, sheesh."

"Can my friends come with me, Tall and Furry?" Halley said.

"Absolutely." The nurse put out his hand. "Jerry."

"This is Ben," Halley said. "He's smarter than he looks."

"He looks pretty smart to me," Jerry said.

Halley held my hand. She was shaking all over. We went into a small room with two recliners and a huge TV. Halley sank back into one of them, and Flip hopped up into her lap and yawned. I learned that dogs yawn when they're tired, sure, but also when they're nervous.

Jerry slid down Halley's shirt a little. The port was right under her collarbone, toward the middle of her chest. It looked like where you connect the air pump to a bike tire, except it was white plastic. Jerry attached a tube that went into a bag of fluid hanging from a metal hook in the wall. The stuff in the bag was clear. It looked like plain old water.

"Here we go, Halley," Jerry said. "Might feel a little cold at first." He unscrewed this little plastic ring in the middle of the tube. He dimmed the lights and clicked on the TV but left the sound off. He handed me the remote. "See you guys in half an hour," he said.

We stared at the TV. It was a Justice League cartoon.

"When last we saw our interstellar travelers Bruce, Helen, and Flip, they were nearing the planet of Mundum Nostrum," Halley said. "Well, now they're almost there. It's in the most beautiful place in the galaxy. So quiet out here. So pink and clean. We're flying right by Sirius now. We're swinging in so close it's all we can see. There's no sky, just the star. You can look right into it, and it doesn't hurt at all.

It burns cool and blue and even Rayburn can't be sad now. There's a breeze, whispery. It's Tess's voice. 'You're so close now,' she says. 'So close.' Ben? I'm not worried."

"Me either," I said.

"I didn't sleep so great with this hairy little bug kicking at me. I'm just gonna close my eyes for a bit, okay? Let's take a nap, the three of us." She closed her eyes. Flip closed his and burrowed under her sweatshirt and she smiled. "This dog," she said with her eyes still closed. "He is so freaking amazing." She looked healthy. Her cheeks were even pink that day. It just didn't make any sense. "You know what?" she said. "On second thought, can you find the music channel and dial up some rap?"

48

I ALWAYS WANTED TO
BE A VAMPIRE

She threw up in the car on the way home. I was in the back
with her and held the bag. Flip didn't mind the smell. He
cuddled right into her and wagged his tail. When we pulled
up to the apartment, Mrs. Lorentz said, "He's a lifesaver,
right Halley?"

"Good job, Flip," I said.

Halley rolled her eyes. "Again, she was talking about *you*,
dope." She threw up as soon as we got into the apartment.
I rubbed her back while she was bent over the toilet. Her
fuzzy orange beret fell into the water. I took it out.

"Sorry," she said.

"I don't mind."

"No, that you have to see me like this. Puking. Bald. I'm
lucky I have a totally gorgeous head."

"You do."

"Oh, I know. Yeah. I always wanted to be a vampire."

"I can't see you ripping apart somebody's neck to suck their blood."

"I wouldn't. I'd be a nice one. I'd be a medical lab technician and drink what they were going to throw away. I will soon, though."

"Become a lab technician?"

"Look like a vampire. You'll see, when I lose more weight. I might cry now. In sixth grade I was voted Best Hair. Me, Halley Lorentz. I'm sure to get into Harvard with that on my application. Okay, I'm actually *not* going to cry, it seems. Phew."

She leaned on me into her room and flopped down onto her bed. "Cover me up fast with all the blankets. Thanks. Ben, I stink and I'm gross, so Flip's the only one who can stay, okay? You're the only one, Flip. His eyes, Ben. See?"

I left them in there. Mrs. Lorentz was passed out on the couch with her arms over her eyes. Mercurious was making soup. "Need any help?" I said.

"You're doing just fine," he said. "On second thought, you can taste this for me."

"Tastes healthy."

He laughed, sort of. Mercurious had a very quiet laugh, more of a smile, the kind the superhero has at the end of the movie, when all is right with the world again. "I'm thinking this might be a little *too* healthy for you and me. How'd you like to order a pizza?"

"I'll go pick it up," I said. "I have to walk Flip anyway."

On the way there I texted Aunt Jeanie that I was going to have to postpone dinner. I had a really busy week coming up.

Halley slept straight through until the next morning. Her mom made her drink some cold peppermint tea with honey, and she threw it up. She slept. By four o'clock Sunday afternoon, she was up. She was too stiff to stay in bed, but too tired to work on *The Magic Box*. We played video games. Her phone buzzed with a text. It had been buzzing practically nonstop.

"They're all demanding to see me now. My friends from school. Yes, believe it or not, I am fantastically popular and just chock-*full* of friends. They've *been* demanding to see me, ever since that first trip to the emergency room last winter, but I keep blowing them off. I know that's mean, not letting them help me, but I can't see them right now, you know? I want to be a hundred and eleven percent. It's not because of the way I look. It's because of the way they'll look at me. That sadness in their eyes. That fear. You and Flip, you guys never look that way. Maybe you look a little sad, but you're not afraid for me."

She was right. I wasn't afraid for her. She was tough enough to handle anything. I was afraid for *me*. Of what it would be like without her, the world. It would be like a planet that lost its orbit and got chucked into space and everything's cold and you can't breathe. "I have a present for you," I said. "It's in the other room."

"Your room?"

"I'll be right back."

It was a rainbow-striped cap. I bought it on the street from the man who sold socks and phone cases by the subway. She put it on her head and checked herself out in the mirror. "I love you, Ben Coffin. I'm never taking it off, even after my hair grows back."

49
WHERE'S HALLEY?

"How's she doing?" Mold said Monday during lunch in our regular spot in the cafeteria.

"She's doing great," I said. The window was open and it was one of those days in early fall when the air forgets it's not summer anymore. Every fly in the city decided to get together that afternoon for a conference around the dumpster.

"I'd like to visit her," Chucky said. "Not to look at her butt. That wouldn't be right at this point."

"It wasn't right at the other point either," I said.

"Coffin, I'm thirteen. You'll understand when you get to be my age. I just want to thank her."

"For *what?*"

"I don't know. She was nice to me."

"She's not going anywhere. You'll see her when she gets better."

"I'd like to come to Read to Rufus again today, just in case.

Sorry. I didn't mean that. I'm sure she's going to be fine."

"Look, Chucky, maybe some other time. I'll talk with her about it. We'll see, okay?"

Angelina plunked down next to me and took one of my Chips Ahoy! Ronda stood behind her, arms folded. "Damon said you lost your mind," Angelina said with her mouth full of my cookie.

"What a brilliant observation by Damon," I said.

"You so did not just talk to me that way. Have you lost your mind?"

"Didn't we just establish that?" Halley inspired me to stand up for myself. The way she was standing up to her cancer. Not hers. It. I took out my phone and took a picture of Angelina. "Pinto said you need to steer clear. Go or I email this to her."

"You freaking geek. If I get suspended—"

"I seriously don't care," I said.

"Let's go," Ronda said.

Angelina got up. "Sorry about your pants," she said to me.

I rolled my eyes. "Okay, and why would you be sorry about my pants?"

"Seems you sat in some gum."

I stood up and sure enough my butt and the bench were attached by a long string of Juicy Fruit, it smelled like. "You're brilliant, Angelina," I said.

"Thank you."

"No, I mean seriously. You are *so* creative. The whole putting gum on somebody's seat thing? It's never been done before. How did you ever come up with such a dazzling idea? I mean, you are a genius."

"Smart enough not to sit on a wad of gum anyway." She was still laughing, like she was genuinely happy about messing me up.

"Shut up, Ange," Ronda said.

"No, seriously, isn't he like the hugest loser?"

"You know what, Caramello? Coffin's right. You're a freaking *genius.* You're not allowed to hang with me anymore." She shoved Angelina and headed off.

Angelina chased after her. "*I'm* not allowed to hang with *you?* You have it all backward, *Glom*ski."

"I hate her," Chucky said. "Seriously, why does Halley have to get cancer when it should be Angelina?"

"Chucky? Shut the freak up."

"What?"

"Why does *either* of them have to get it?" I couldn't erase it from my mind, the image of Halley's fuzzy orange beret floating in the toilet.

When I got to the library for Read to Rufus, Flip and Mercurious were there, but Mrs. Lorentz and Halley weren't. "Is she okay?" I said.

"She has a temperature," Mercurious said. "Are *you* okay?"

"Of course," I said.

"She wants us to take pictures. She says to tell everybody she'll be here next time for sure."

And that's what we did. Still, Brian asked, "But where is she? Why can't she be with us?"

Flip seemed confused too. He kept looking around the room for her.

When we got back to the apartment I showed her the pictures. She kept going through them. "I'm starting to feel better. I feel it working, the medicine, you know? I *feel* it. I'll be at the next one. I will, Ben."

"Oh, I know you will."

"For sure."

"For sure."

50
IT'S LIKE WHEN YOU BITE YOUR TONGUE

Halley barely said anything during Tuesday breakfast and she didn't eat. "Sweetheart, have some toast at least," Mrs. Lorentz said.

"I'm fine."

"I thought you were feeling better," her mom said.

"I was. But now that I know I'm going to be puking like a maniac in a few hours, I'd rather not waste food." Her second chemotherapy session was that afternoon.

"Halley," her mom said, and that was as far as she got.

"Mom, can't you just shut up for like two *seconds*." She pushed away from the table and stomped to her room and slammed the door. Flip scratched on it and she let him in.

It was weird, seeing her talk to her mom that way. It made me think she was really worried, which got me really worried. "Can I go with her to chemotherapy?" I said.

"No, you can help her by going to school and doing well on your social studies test," Mrs. Lorentz said.

I got back from school a little before Halley got home from chemotherapy. Again she went right into the bathroom and threw up. Again I rubbed her back while she puked. Nothing came up, just dry heaves. "Can you put my cap back on?" she said. She liked to wear it backward.

Flip wiggled between her and the toilet bowl and slumped and sighed.

"This is true friendship," she said.

"He's awesome," I said.

"Ben, how can you not know I'm talking about you? Idiot. I'm going to Read to Rufus tomorrow. I am." She heaved again, and then again.

I helped her to her bed. She crashed on it. I took her shoes off and put all her blankets on her. I left Flip with her and I didn't see her until right before I went to bed. I had to take Flip out for his last walk. I cracked the door to let him out, and I looked in to see if she was okay. Her mom was reading to her, but Halley was sleeping. Mrs. Lorentz came out with Flip. She walked with us. "Your aunt Jeanie called," she said. "She thought you were avoiding her, until I told her about Halley. Ben, are you avoiding her?"

"No. Maybe."

"I want you to go to dinner with her. I'd invite her over, but with Halley so sick, well, you know. When Halles is better, we'll have a party. I want Jeanie to be there, okay?"

"Okay."

"Meanwhile, can you give her a call? Please, for me, all right?"

Wednesday morning Halley was awake and dressed before I was. She was making Flip's breakfast. "I'm taking him for his walk," she said.

Her mom frowned. She put her hand on Halley's forehead. "Sit," she said.

"Mom—"

"Halley Lorentz, sit down. If your temperature's fine you can walk Flip." She went through this tray where we kept all Halley's medical stuff: the blood pressure cuff, the stethoscope, these pills to make her less queasy, these other pills to help with her headaches, a couple of thermometers. Mrs. Lorentz popped one under Halley's tongue.

"This isn't the butt one, right?" Halley said.

"Of *course* not. Sheesh."

"She's so not sure," Halley said to me.

We waited for the thermometer to stop rising. Flip poked Halley's leg with his nose to make her watch him do this trick where he stood on his hind legs and sort of moonwalked backward. Even in her crummy mood, she laughed. She took the thermometer out. "See? Perfect." She grabbed Flip's leash and ran out with him.

Mrs. Lorentz checked the thermometer and frowned. "Ben, go with her. Make sure she doesn't pass out in the middle of the freaking boardwalk," except she didn't say "freaking."

By the time I got to the elevator, she was gone. I took the stairs down to the lobby. She hadn't even made it to the front door. She and Flip were sitting on the bench by the mailboxes. I sat next to her. She was shaking. "Don't say anything," she said.

"I won't."

"I'm not scared."

"I know."

"This is just the medicine working. It's strong, so of course it's going to be knocking me out."

"I know."

"Yeah." She caught her breath. "He kisses me awake in the mornings, Flip."

"He does that."

"Uh-huh. It's too quiet here, but I'll tell you."

"Tell me what?"

"It's called rhabdomyosarcoma. There, I said it. Even the name sounds disgusting enough to make you want to puke, right? Sounds evil? Except it's not. I'm not saying it's good either. It's just like every other living thing, trying to survive. It's simply being what it is, which is a tumor that worms through your guts and then the rest of you like an exploded bowl of spaghetti. Or at least that's what the one they took out of me last winter was going to do. Nobody told me that, but I read it online, in one of the chat rooms. This boy a little older than me said that's what the tumor in him was up to. You want to know what it feels like too, right? Most times, I don't feel it. And then I do. This warmth that's almost a burn, and then it goes away. And then sometimes it's something *completely* different. Like last night it snuck up on me and pounced. You ever bite your tongue? It was like that, except all over my body. Now I'm sorry I talked about it. Talking about it gives it power. I need to keep my focus on the golden stuff. Let's go."

"Halley."

"Back upstairs, I mean. Let's go back upstairs. I have to go to bed. I'm freezing. Sorry Flip." She hung heavy on me in the elevator. "Ben, you don't have to say anything. There's nothing to say. Just hold my hand. Thanks. Your hand's almost warm. It feels really good."

51
FLIP'S MAGIC

She didn't make it to Read to Rufus that time either. Afterward I gathered everybody together, the kids, parents, and teachers. We walked to the beach. It was a beautiful day. We made a get-well video full of stuff we thought might make her laugh. The kids made goofy faces, inside-out eyelids, huge balls of fake snot made from chewed-up paper, dripping out of their noses. One of the teachers was a gymnast a long time ago, and she did a split and ripped her pants up the butt. One kid hid behind another except for her arms, so the kid in front looked like she had four arms. One of the dads spun his four-year-old daughter in circles and then put her down on the ground, and she was so dizzy she giggled and staggered around off balance like she was drunk. Flip thought she wanted to dance with him, so he did his moonwalk thing.

They all left video messages saying "Feel better" and "We miss you." Brian's video to her was, "Ben said you promised you'd watch me read again. If you come I'll give you a real long hug and I'll let you kiss me on the cheek, even though I already have a girlfriend."

I went back to the library and uploaded the videos and edited them. When I got back to the Lorentzes' Halley was still in bed but awake and sitting up. She was making a sketch of the Golden Tower of Light as it was about to dock with an antenna on top of Mundum Nostrum's tallest skyscraper.

"Hey," I said.

"Hey."

"It was awesome today."

"I'm sure."

"Everybody misses you." I handed her my phone. "We made a video for you."

She handed me her iPad. More charts, more numbers. "It means it isn't working, the chemotherapy. Not at all." She rolled away. "I have to go to sleep." I put my hand on her shoulder but she shrugged it off. She cried so hard I thought she'd die of shortness of breath. Flip wiggled into her arms and nudged her chin, and she started to calm down. She whispered things to him and then she got quiet and wiped her eyes and hugged him and he snuggled her, and I left them like that.

Mrs. Lorentz was on the phone, pacing up and down the kitchen. She said, "But what about the experimental drug?

You said it looked promising. Then there's still hope." Mercurious was in the dining room, working on the model of Luna Park 1905. I sat next to him. "I could use some help with this," he said. "You have time to give me a hand?"

"Sure," I said, and we worked on the model together. I painted the smaller buildings with gold dots and put flags on them. Mercurious was hanging a crescent moon.

The next morning I delivered my coupons alone. Flip was spending all his time with Halley now, and I was glad. When he was with her she was calm and smiled more.

The air was cold, and I whipped through my route and got the deliveries done before sunrise. By the time I was back at the apartment, Halley and Flip were at the breakfast table. She still looked pretty sick, but she was grinning. Flip kept pulling off her socks. She was watching the video we made for her. "I won't miss the next one," she said.

"I know," I said.

"Meanwhile, I need you to help Dad tomorrow night. It's the huge bar mitzvah at the Museum of Natural History. I was supposed to assist. I was going to try, but Mom wants me to rest up before we get into this new chemotherapy thing. Dad says not to ask you, that he'll be able to manage, because he knows the whole magician thing freaks you out. But I told him you're a big boy and ready to face your fears and you'd love to help him. He's unveiling a new illusion. He's been working on it for the past year. It'll be spectacular when he pulls it off. Congratulations, you've been promoted to magician's assistant." She snapped her fingers, and the sun just peeked over the horizon and nailed us with a gold beam.

"How'd you do that?" I said.

She spun the iPad around. It was on the weather page. Right at the top was sunrise: 6:55 a.m. Right above that was the time of day: 6:55 a.m. "I actually think I might be able to stomach half a waffle this morning," she said.

"Cool," I said, and I made us waffles.

That afternoon Aunt Jeanie picked me up and we headed out to the diner. "I don't want you to feel like you have to do this," I said. "You know, us hanging out because you think that's what Mom would want."

"But *I* want to. Do you?"

I nodded and forced myself to fake a smile.

She patted my hand, and then she took her hand away. "Yes. Well, Leo wanted me to, to tell you he's sorry. He really did. He really is."

I nodded. "How is he, like, doing?"

"Oh Ben, you're so sweet. I'm touched, really. He's going to be okay. I'll let him know you asked about him." She chewed her bottom lip for a bit. "Do you mind if I ask how Halley's doing?"

"No, not at all. She's doing great. Seriously. They're putting her on a new medicine, and it's going to do the trick."

"I'm sure," she said.

"It is. Really."

"Oh, I know."

52
HALLEY'S STARDUST
AND RAINBOW SNOW

Mercurious and I finished up our last rehearsal Friday afternoon in his workshop in the church basement. "Ready?" he said.

"I'm a little freaked, but I think I got it."

"A little freaked is good. We just need to fix you up with one last thing." He gave me a sparkly purple sweat suit.

We got there right as the museum closed, and the party started right after that. The guests packed into the Hall of Ocean Life. We'd set up the show the night before, and now all we could do was wait until after dinner, when Mercurious would pull off his grandest illusion yet.

The kid whose bar mitzvah it was came over and introduced himself and gave me the same gift bag his friends were getting. It had all the stuff I loved: vintage comics, a chronograph watch with a flashlight and about ten pounds of candy. He took me over to the buffet to make sure I ate. "I was really nervous to meet your dad," he said.

I didn't bother to correct him about the fact that Mercurious wasn't my dad. He was, well, Mercurious. "Why?"

"Ben, dude, he's totally famous. You're gonna be a magician too, right? You get to be at a party every night."

It really was an awesome party. Think of being able to run around the Museum of Natural History while eating mini pizzas and shooting your friends with laser guns. Then it was showtime.

The lights went down and I went to my spot in the video projection booth. Mercurious went out into the middle of the hall and the place went silent. "Jon, would you come up here? I'd like to introduce you to your guardian angel."

"I didn't know I had one," the bar mitzvah boy said.

"We all do. As you begin your journey into this next magical phase of your life, know that you always have someone looking out for you." Mercurious tapped Jon's shoulder, and Halley appeared, a miniature version of her, the way she looked almost a year ago, the first time I met her, at the library, when she was helping out behind the counter, and she rolled her eyes when I gave her *I, Robot* to check out for me. Here though, now, in the museum, her long, light brown hair was pulled back into a braided bun, with silver cords woven through. She wore a rainbow-colored gown with angel's wings.

Mercurious made Jon hold out his hand, and Halley fluttered down into his palm. She raised her own palm and blew stardust into Jon's face. She vanished and reappeared life-size on top of the ninety-four-foot model of the blue whale. She knelt down from the whale's fin and blew stardust. It rained from the ceiling onto the guests. It was snowing silver and pink and gold and emerald, and I remembered the time my mom wanted to go to the beach during a snowstorm. We bundled up and drank hot chocolate from a thermos, and the strangest thing happened. It was still snowing, but the sun came out, just for a minute, just long enough to turn the flakes every color of the rainbow.

Somebody called out to me from far away, like the voice was coming through radio static, and it was. It was Mercurious. *"Ben, can you hear me?"* He was on the private channel of our walkie-talkies.

"Ten-four, Mercurious."

"I just wanted to let you know that I think your mom's watching, and she's proud of you. We all are. Thank you, son. I really needed you here with me tonight." And I saw through the stardust that down on the floor, he was looking up at Halley's ghost, and the tear tracks were zigzags on his cheeks. I tried not to get too freaked out. I mean, if Mercurious was worried, then there definitely was a reason to worry now.

We finished loading up the projectors into Mercurious's SUV. "Put out your palm," he said. He put five hundred-dollar bills into it. "That's crazy," I said.

"That's your share."

"But all I did was play around on the iPad." It was like a video game. I moved Halley's image here and there and made sure the video projectors went on and off at the right times. "I had too much fun to make this much money."

"Ben, that's how it's supposed to be."

"Two questions. First, can you put this into my college fund?"

"I like the way you think. What else?"

"When can we do the next one?"

Flip met us at the door. Mrs. Lorentz wasn't far behind. She'd been crying but now she was smiling. "How'd it go?" she said.

"Awesome," I said. "How's Halley?"

"Awesome. Truly. Halley is absolutely amazing." She was talking to Mercurious when she said that last part. Mercurious frowned. "Go in and say hi, Ben," Mrs. Lorentz said. "She's been waiting up for you. She'll want to hear all about tonight."

Flip led me into her room and hopped onto her bed and yawned.

"How'd I do?" she said. "All the boys said I was hot, right? Let's see the gift bag." She chucked the comics and grabbed the flashlight watch and put it on. "While you were out making me fly around the Museum of Natural History, I figured out the next chapter of *The Magic Box*."

"Okay?"

"So as the Golden Tower of Light coasts into Mundum Nostrum, a series of miniature asteroids comes out of nowhere."

"They always do. Better activate the laser shields."

"Unfortunately, the laser shields aren't going to be enough this time. These asteroids are tiny but insidiously lethal. They snuck completely undetected into the ship's orbit and they're moving too fast. Think of a bag of frozen peas traveling at supersonic speed. They blow right through the laser shields and explode when they hit the Golden Tower of Light. The back of the ship is gone, completely shorn away. Now, in the *front* of the ship, Rayburn is tucked safely into his sleeping pod. Flip is tucked safely into the backpack on our hero Bruce's back. Bruce is secured to the ship by a golden tendril of light. Helen, on the other hand, was floating free in zero gravity when the asteroids hit. She's being sucked out of the ship, into the vacuum of space. So is the magic box. Helen grabs it and jams it into a crack in the fuselage just before she flies outward into the perfect infinity of the stars."

"Bruce goes with her—"

"No, Bruce stays with the ship."

"Absolutely *not*. Unacceptable. Bruce follows Helen—"

"Bruce has to bring the magic box to Tess. He has to deliver the Greatest Treasure and save the people of Mundum Nostrum. He has to keep on keeping on."

"But what if he doesn't want to, not without Helen?"

"He forces himself to realize how strong he is, how awesome. He's a traveler, like Tess always told him he was. That's what he's born to do. Halley will always be with Ben and Flip anyway. Helen, I mean. Helen will always be with them."

"How? Just explain to me how the frick Halley is with them when they're stuck on Mundum Nostrum and Halley's . . . just . . . *not.*"

She held my hand. "I can't do it again, Ben. I can't be sick like that anymore. Me and Mom were on the phone with the doctors all night. This new drug they were thinking of is totally experimental. It has a twenty percent chance of giving me another three months. There's a fifty percent chance it will kill me in three days. There's a hundred percent chance it will make me sicker than I've ever felt in my life."

"What about other stuff, like surgery?"

"Not an option. Ben, they found it in my blood vessels. It's only a matter of time before it spreads everywhere."

"I don't know what to say."

"I don't either, really." She brushed the hair out of my eyes. "It's the weirdest thing. I mean, I knew back in the winter, after they took out the tumor, that the kind I have is the worst kind. But I really thought I was gonna beat it. The five-year survival rate in children under fourteen is thirty percent. Almost one in three. I thought I was going to be the one. I was so sure, I even started to feel bad about it. About being the one who lives when the other two would have to die. You ever wonder that? Why somebody has to die? Why we all do? It just seems so crazy." Flip pawed her to pet him. She did. "The doctor said now that I won't be on chemotherapy, I'll actually feel a little better for a little while. I'm not giving up, Ben Coffin, and you can't either. I don't know how many days I have left—fifty, thirty, seventy—but we're going to fight to be happy every minute we get to spend with each other. The happier we are now, the happier we'll always be when you remember me. I need you to have my back on this one."

"Okay," I said. "Okay, I do."

"Promise?"

"Swear." We locked pinkies.

"Good," she said. At first I thought it was weird, her being so calm after just finding out she was going to die sooner rather than later. But then I saw it wasn't calmness. She was just plain tired. Her eyelids were heavy and dark. She looked beat-up. "You look like you want to ask me something," she said.

I wanted to ask her lots of things. Like, Who could I be mad at? Seriously, why couldn't the cancer have an inventor, some psycho villain along the lines of Darth Sidious, somebody I could track down and beat the crud out of before I stabbed him in the heart with my laser sword, except how can you do that when the traitor doesn't have a heart? My biggest question was, Why couldn't it be me instead of her? "The magic box," I said. "Once and for all, what's inside?"

She mussed my hair a little, and just after she'd fixed it too. "I promise I won't leave you hanging. You'll find out soon enough."

53

MRS. SALVADOR AND
PEACOCK FEATHERS

Halley never really bounced back from being tired from the chemotherapy. She slept a lot, but she wasn't nauseous anymore, and she said she wasn't in pain—most of the time. By the middle of October, though, they gave her pills to help her hurt less. Mrs. Lorentz made me and Mercurious stick to our schedules, and for me that meant school, homework, my coupon deliveries, Read to Rufus, and keeping up with Aunt Jeanie, which, to be honest, was the hardest thing. Or the second-hardest thing.

Mrs. Lorentz took a leave of absence from the library to take care of Halley. A nurse came for a few hours a day to help out too. She was super nice, Mrs. Salvador, and she loved to read to Halley. She was going for a degree in literature at the City College of New York, and that's why the agency paired her with us. Halley loved the way she read *Feathers*. She acted out the parts and did voices and stuff.

When Halley was sleeping, Mrs. Salvador and I talked. "How do you stand it?" I said. "Having to say good-bye to one patient, and then starting all over again?"

"It's a gift each time I meet someone new," she said. Flip took a break from cuddle duty to be with us and climbed into Mrs. Salvador's lap. He rolled belly up for a scratch and wagged his tail and yipped until she gave him what he wanted. "And anyway, they never really say good-bye. Right Flip?"

The third weekend of October Mercurious and I were on a long line at Costco with a cart full of stuff for Halley, ginger ale and bright plants for her windowsill. She liked to sit with her sketchbook and look out at the beach and Luna Park. We had other stuff in the cart too, lots of paper towels and sani wipes and yes, diapers. An old man on the next line had the same ones in his cart, and he looked like us, sort of like he couldn't believe any of this was actually happening.

"How did you guys meet?" I said to Mercurious.

"Penny and I? We were in the same library sciences program."

"What made you switch to magic?"

"I guess I never thought of it as a switch. You ever think about going into it? Library science? I think you'd be great at it. You're analytical and you have a huge heart."

Talking about what I wanted to do when I grew up felt

weird when my best friend was never going to grow up. "I'd like to be you," I said.

"A party magician?" he said doubtfully.

"A great guy."

"Ben, you're something else," he said, which is exactly what my mom used to say except she'd never tell me exactly what that something else was.

When we got back, Halley was feeling pretty good. She was sitting up at the window with Flip and bossing us around about where she wanted the flowers. We moved the model of Luna Park into her room. There wasn't much left to do before it'd be finished. We had to put in a walkway, so the people could get into the golden tower. Mercurious wanted to hang a few planets over it too, and a handful of stars. Mrs. Lorentz stuck fake peacock feathers into Halley's rainbow cap.

That night on my way to the kitchen for a midnight peanut butter and jelly and milk I found Mrs. Lorentz and Mercurious passed out on the couch with a photo album. They'd left the window open a crack and I could smell the ocean. They looked cold, so I put a blanket on them.

54

FRIENDS AND KITES

The texts and calls got to be too much, so she set aside a day to let everybody visit. She posted a sign on her door: NO CRYING. YES LAUGHING. Practically everybody got it backward.

They knew she had that sweet tooth, and they brought her cakes, cookies, and barrels of gummy bears, none of which she could eat because she'd pretty much stopped eating. They brought her stuffed animals, which Flip collected in a corner of her room, like they were his harem. Chucky brought flowers. "You think these are good enough? They're only from the deli. I wanted to get twelve but I was starving and if I didn't get a meatball parm I seriously would have died of starvation. I only had enough money left for like six."

"What are they?"

"Posies. Or maybe pansies, I don't know. Do I look like a horticulturalist?"

"You look like you're about to cry. Chucky, you better not."

"I *won't*, Coffin. Chill."

I brought him in. Halley said to Chucky, "You forgot your pocket protector."

"I try not to wear it at non-school events, except in extraordinary circumstances."

"Those being?"

"For instance if I'm somewhere that requires multiple pens. Sometimes I go to autograph shows, and the superhero or whoever steals your Bic. You were the first girl who didn't call me a dork." He cried. He gave her the flowers.

"Poppies," she said. She cried. "Chucky, can you give Ben and me a minute?"

He sobbed his way out.

"Get everybody out," she said. "I'm sorry, but I can't stand it. I'll say my good-byes on Facebook. I only want to be with you and Flip from here on in, Mom and Mercurious. And the Read to Rufus kids. I'm saying those good-byes in person, if it's the last thing I do."

"What's the difference, Mom? I mean, we're really worried about my cold getting worse at this point?"

"Let's try again," Mrs. Salvador said. She put the digital thermometer into Halley's ear.

It was one of those perfect October afternoons, deep blue sky and a beach wind that puffed up the ocean into whitecaps. The kites were all over the sky. Halley wanted to go out and watch.

Mrs. Salvador checked the thermometer. She frowned.

"Can't do it, Halles," her mom said. "I don't want to be the bad guy."

"Then don't be."

"You go outside on a day like today and it might be your last day."

"So? Why do you have to be such a freaking psycho about every little thing?"

"You know what? I'm sick of your nastiness to me. Go to your room until you remember how to talk to me."

"Fine." She went and shut the door as hard as she could, and we could still hear her crying and screaming "I hate you" over and over on the other side of it. Then Mrs. Lorentz started crying and Mrs. Salvador said, "Okay. Okay. Everybody breathe now."

"Ben?" Halley said from behind her door. "Ben!"

I went in. She was on her bed, facing the wall. Flip was dragging a stuffed animal across the floor to her. She reached back for me to grab her hand. "Promise me I'll get to be outside one last time."

"Promise."

"I guess having cancer doesn't make me immune from being a jerk now and again. Tell Mom I know I'm being an idiot."

55
WHOA

That third Wednesday of October was a warm day. Mrs. Lorentz wanted to drive Halley over to the library, but she wanted to walk. Mercurious sided with Halley and said they would meet us over there. I brought the wheelchair just in case. She made it a couple of blocks before she needed to use the chair. Still, she was psyched. She couldn't wait to see Brian. His teacher emailed Halley that Brian was close to reading at grade level now.

Mrs. Lorentz and Mrs. Salvador had wrapped up Halley in all her crazy colorful scarves. She gave them away to the kids. Brian read to her and Flip, and she got her hug and kiss on the cheek. The kids were cool. They didn't make her sad. They knew she was dying, but they said good-bye like they'd see her next week, and I swear they meant what they said, and I really wished I could be like them.

After, she wanted to ride down the boardwalk, just her,

me, and Flip. She wanted me to push the wheelchair fast. "Push, Coffin. *Push*. Faster. Yeah, like that. Woohoo!"

We were in her room, sunset. We worked on the model of Luna Park 1905, or I worked, and she watched. I fiddled with a string of lights that went from the top of the golden tower to one of the stars Mercurious had hung from the ceiling. Flip snored in her lap. "Ready for the last chapter of *The Magic Box*?" she said.

I'd been waiting for her to bring it up, or more like dreading it. I didn't want the story to end. "Ready," I said.

"Tess says, 'You've saved Mundum Nostrum, Ben. You and Flip. You brought the magic. Herein lies the cure to every malady, the fix for Rayburn's sadness, the peace that will help the people of Mundum Nostrum remember they are of one blood, brothers and sisters, friends forever. Go ahead and see for yourself, the Greatest Treasure.' Tess gives him the box. He opens it. He looks in. 'That's it?' he says. 'That's everything,' Tess says."

"And?" I said.

"And that's all," Halley said. "End of story."

"Uh, *no*. After dragging me and Flip all the way to Mundum Nostrum, you're telling me what's inside that box."

"Seriously, Coffin? You haven't figured it out yet? By the way, if you're ever going to kiss me, you might want to do it soon. For instance, now would be a good time."

"Way to distract me from trying to get you to tell me

once and for all what's inside the stupid box. Plus, I thought you said there's nothing better than friends."

"Forget what I said."

I kissed her. I felt her heartbeat in her lips. They were chapped, and then they got slippery. They were just like I'd dreamed, lit with sparks. All the while Flip snored right next to us in the upside-down flying squirrel pose. "Whoa," I said.

"Yeah, whoa. We're shaking like crazy, aren't we?"

"I can't stop my teeth from chattering."

"Was that your first kiss?" she said.

"Yours too?"

"Third. Ha. Be happy for me."

"Did I do it right?" I said. "Like, was it lame, ours, compared to the other two?"

"Kiss me again and I'll tell you."

"Halley?"

"Ben?"

"I totally freaking love you."

"Me freaking too."

I woke the next morning to Flip's barking and Halley's screaming and then Mrs. Lorentz's. I could barely hear Mercurious as he called 911, even though I was standing right next to him. Halley bunched up like a pill bug. "It's cold but it burns," she said. "My back, in the middle. Like somebody's hitting me."

The EMTs came and put her onto a stretcher. "My hat," she said. "My rainbow hat. Please." They went lights and sirens to the hospital. Mrs. Lorentz rode with her in the ambulance. By the time Mercurious and I got to the hospital a few minutes after the ambulance, she was on the operating table. She had to have emergency surgery because her kidneys were all blocked up and she couldn't pee. She never made it out of the surgery. One of the nurses said it was a blessing that she didn't drag on for the next few weeks, all drugged up and all but dead. Yes, that she died in her sleep was a gift. It sure didn't feel like one. Not at all. It was like with Mom all over again. I was so mad. She never told me what was inside the magic box.

56
GOOD-BYE FOR A WHILE

When we got back to the apartment Flip was waiting for me at the front door with one of Halley's dirty socks, I thought, but it was mine. "Flip," I said, and his tail flicked. I crouched and he crawled into my lap. I carried him into Mercurious's office and set him on the couch. I stared at my Chewie poster. Mrs. Lorentz and Mercurious came in. They sat on either side of me. Mrs. Lorentz kissed my forehead.

"Can Flip stay?" I said.

"What are you talking about?" she said.

"Everybody I love disappears. I can't figure out how to bring them back. I have to go now."

"What?"

"I'll remind you of her. It's just going to make you feel worse."

"Ben, reminding us of her is going to keep her alive," Mrs. Lorentz said. "How can you say these things to us? How can you not see that this is where you're supposed to be, you and Flip? We're not losing you too. We're *not*. My Ben. Oh God, please don't go. Please. We need each other. We really do. Michael, tell him. *Tell* him."

Mercurious put his arm over my shoulder. He went somewhere between hug and headlock, just like Mom used to. "She left something for you," he said. "Come on now, son." I followed him into Halley's room, and Flip followed me. We stood in front of her desk, in front of the model of Luna Park 1905 spread over it. We'd come so close to finishing it, just one last detail. I'd wanted to put some people in the top of the tower, a family looking out over the city, the ocean.

Mercurious opened the desk drawer and took out Halley's phone and gave it to me in its bright pink case. He patted my back and left his hand there for a bit, and then he left. The phone was tapped up to Halley's notepad. I sat in the desk chair and read the note written three days before, the time stamp said.

> Dear Ben,
>
> As awesome as our story of *The Magic Box* is, it's not as
> awesome as your story, and that's the one I want you to tell.
> Speaking of *The Magic Box* . . . It's right there, in the model,
> in *Dreamland at Night*. Mercurious snuck it in for me. Look
> at the Golden Tower of Light. You see the foundation there,
> the one the tower is built on? You can look inside now, Ben.
> Yup, there's the Greatest Treasure. I still can't believe you didn't
> figure it out. The secret was in Flip's big gold eyes all along.

Your mom knew too. It's why she picked you.

Take care of Mom and Dad for me, and give my books to

Housing Works.

Love forever and ever,

Rainbow Girl

I lifted the golden tower out of the model of Luna Park 1905. Beneath it was a wooden box, just big enough to keep a book safe. I opened the box. Inside was a mirror. I looked into it, and all I saw was me.

57

TRAVELERS AND MAGICIANS

My favorite thing about Halley Lorentz will always be this: Every time she hugged you it was like she hadn't seen you in a long, long time. I'll never forget the way she held hands either, cold and trembly and hard enough to make your fingers ache a little the next day. Frannie's teacher from *Feathers* was right after all. Some things never fade away.

It's a year later and I go to a different school now, one for science geeks. It's really competitive and I'm not, but otherwise it's awesome. I never fall asleep in class and nobody smacks me in the back of the head. The only fights I get into are about whether or not roentgenium can occur naturally in environments where the gravity is a hundred and eleven times stronger than it is on Earth. If I stay on track I have a shot at getting into a good engineering program for college. Then again I might just go ahead and be a waterslide tester. Most of all, I like working with Mercurious. Maybe I'll design rockets and roller coasters by day and be a magician at night.

Aunt Jeanie and I get together a couple of times a month. She's always giving me presents, really nice stuff from Macy's, and some of it's even stuff that I like to wear. Hoodies and jeans and stuff. I tell her I feel bad, her spending all this money, but she says I shouldn't worry because she gets it dirt-cheap with her discount. She never brings up Leo unless I ask, and I do once in a while. He isn't drinking and he's losing weight, she says. She never asks me if I want to see him, because she knows I don't. I want him to be okay, though. I really, really do.

This one sweater Jeanie got me—it's really preppy. I wear it when Flip and I do Read to Rufus. Brian is reading above grade level now, and he isn't afraid to be caught carrying around a book.

I posted *The Magic Box* on some of the story sites. All told it has a little over eleven hundred reviews so far. A few girls and one guy even wrote spinoffs of it and a few more were threatening to. That's all Halley ever wanted anyway. To give the story to a few people. I posted her sketches too, with the story. I listen to the audio tracks, the notes Halley talked into her phone. I loved the sound of her voice. I still love it, loud and husky and just plain true.

It's Saturday, and Flip and I meet up with Chucky at the basketball courts. We both totally blow and these bigger dudes kick us off the court, which is fine because my asthma is starting up and Chucky is sucking wind worse than me because he's been eating way too many donuts. "Want to come over for my sister's birthday party?" he says.

"Can't, have to help Mercurious. Which sister and how old, though?"

"Coffin, are you serious? I'm lucky if I can remember their names."

Mercurious and I head on over to the hospital. We're in the pediatric wing where the kids are all bunched up in this one room, and they're going *whoa* and *holy crud, did you see that?* The angel Halley makes her appearance and flutters around the room and kisses each one of them on the cheek. And then Mercurious calls me out from behind the video controls for the showstopper. It's an old trick, but the kids go bonkers for it. I take off my magic silver sombrero and put it on the table and tap it with my light saber. Flip pops out in his rabbit ears and surfs on over to the kids and knuckle bumps them. There's high-fours all around and all the kids are cracking up and in the corner Mom Lorentz is crying but more she's laughing too.

After the show it's such a nice night, way too nice to be inside. Flip and I head out. We stop off at that supermarket where the lady gave me the cheddar samples that brought us all together in the first place, and I actually *buy* some cheese, and Flip and I head to the beach to play chase.

At dusk we stroll down the boardwalk to Luna Park. The lights are coming on, millions of them. I'm falling hard into my dream, traveling into the past, to 1905. Somewhere in time it still exists, and an apprentice electrician and a magician watch a young woman swing on the trapeze high into the night sky, and they pray she'll be okay. In the middle of it all is the golden tower. Flip and I run up those winding stairs to the top, and I'm breathless. She's there. She really is. Mom. Laura's with her. Jeanie and, yes, Leo, and it's okay, I don't mind. Then there's the woman who regretted selling Flip for forty dollars, who trained Flip to be awesomeness. The bus driver who fed me. Jerry the chemotherapy nurse, Franco, Mrs. Salvador, Kayla, the Santa magician, even Rayburn. And then there's Halley. Halley most of all.

Flip leaps to greet her and gets his stinky tongue up into her mouth. She holds my hand and we turn to the ocean, and what a view. It's not just the past anymore that I see. It's the future too and it's now and it's everything and everyone I've ever met and will meet. I look out and see forever. Yes, Halley's with me. All I have to do is close my eyes and think of her.

ACKNOWLEDGMENTS

Thank you to Jodi Reamer, who's not only one of the nicest people I know in publishing but also one of the nicest people I know. Do NOT get into a fight with her, though. She'll totally kick your butt. Seriously, she's crazy strong and just plain crazy. Ditto for Alec Shane, who, in addition to being a great agent, is also a great guy. David Levithan, for hooking me up with The Blackbelt.

My Behind The Book crew for hooking me up with the amazing Patty McCormick. The phenomenal Andy Griffiths, for giving the book to the phenomenal Markus Zusak. The lovely Steph Stepan, for giving the book to the lovely Rebecca Stead. The incredibly kind Rick Margolis, for giving the book to The King, aka Gary Schmidt. The wonderful Jacqueline Woodson, for letting me quote *Feathers*, and, for reaching out to Jackie, the divine Nancy Paulsen, who also happens to have a divine singing voice. David Baldacci and Kristen for the nicest tweet and for so many hours of reading happiness—same goes for Timothy Zahn. (Harper Lee and *To Kill a* freaking *Mockingbird* are pretty good too.)

Mary Kate McDevitt and Dani Calotta for the ridiculously beautiful cover; Jasmin Rubero and Regina Castillo for making the inside just as ridiculously beautiful.

Namrata Tripathi, for her perfect notes, her generosity re the cover and for coming up with the most gorgeous title in concert with Ellen Cormier, who gave equally perfect notes, made me crack up (laughing), put up with my lame pranks and generally held my hand as this book made its way through production. Puffin Julia gave rockin' notes too, as did my pal Heather Alexander.

Lauri Hornik, for that final round of notes and the best hugs, for the hilarious late-night e-mails, for taking me to yummy places to eat and for just being so completely and totally awesome to me these many years.

Sheila Hennessey—I don't even know what to say about Sheila, except you know how Ben takes in scruffy little Flip off the street? That's what Sheila did with me. Hugs to Shark. Shout-out to Steve Kent, Doni Kay, JD, Colleen, Ev and Nicole too. Eileen and Dana, Kendra, Stacey B and Kathy D, Mary Raymond, Helen, Kim and Draga, Michael, Penny, Steph, Alaina and my Text peeps. Jen Loja was awesome with cover and title support. Erin, Emily, Alexis, Don, Felicia, Carmela, Venessa, Melinda, Courtney, Anna, Jackie, Jennifer, and Marisa. Steve Meltzer, did you move? How come I don't see you in Frank's anymore? I miss you Jess, Marie, Emily, Scottie, Donne, Sara, Alex.

For the very fun and very marathon phone calls, Shawn Goodman (great man), Gayle Forman (outrageously magnificent), Nan Mercado (guardian angel of punk writers, or at least this one) and my bud Barry Lyga, who also sold me his phone for half what he could have gotten for it on Swappa. Morgan Baden, for keeping Barry on a leash, albeit with limited effectiveness. Michael Northrop, Coe Booth (Coe, might I ask, what are you working on now?), Gordon Korman and the rest of the TARN revelers. Jess, Karlan, Claudio and LIT. Greg Neri, Melissa Walker, Matt de la Peña, Libba Bray, Paul Volponi, Ted Goeglein, Torrey "Brando" Maldonado, Allen Zadoff, and especially Elizabeth Hill and Scott Smith, an amazing friend.

Dad, for always reading; Mom, for always buying. General Kathleen Whelan for marshaling the troops. Baba for all those hours at the *hotokesama*, Kari for all those hours keeping us giggling.

My dogs, Ray (Liotta), Al (Pacino), Bobby (DeNiro), Marty (Scorsese), Nice Guy Eddie (from *Reservoir Dogs*, also the model for Flip. See him there, in the picture with Halley's hand and the magic square?), and my lovely, dainty little jackal MiMi (from *La Bohème*. We needed a lady to class up the joint).

My friends who invite me to their bookstores, libraries, detention centers, schools and crazy conferences, with particular—and particularly fun—craziness coming from that Texas librarian posse and my Florida FAME peeps. JLG crew: love you all.

My friends who visit me every time I close my eyes and think of them.

My editor, Kate Harrison. Kate, your big-hearted and brilliant notes and letters, our calls and lunches and brainstorming sessions—every minute I get with you is the greatest treasure. Our collaborations are so fun I feel guilty getting paid for them. (Please don't tell Lauri I said that.) Thank you for keeping me around all these years. They mean everything to me—your guidance, your teaching, your friendship.

TWO NOTES: The Coney Island Library is a little different from the way I described it here, but it's a dream world for sure. You should go.

Alas, Boardwalk Flight closed in 2014, but it lives on in my heart and can in yours too. All you have to do is close your eyes and think of it, right? (Or, if you're lazy like me—I am—you can search Google images.)